Smarahaim

A Tale of Smidgeon

T. D. Lacey

© PeaChi Publishing
www.peachip.co.uk
Morants Court ◆ Chevening
Kent, United Kingdom

First published 2017

ISBN: 978-0-9928968-2-9

Contents

Foreword

A Smidge is the size of a hornet or a very large bee.

large bee

On soft and breezy summer evenings, you may see them flying above and around lakes and tarns. To the untrained eye, they take on the appearance of large gnats, yet to some (mainly the well-educated Irish folk and the farming communities of Southern England and France) they are called "Midges". They are in fact "Smidge" or "Smidgeon".

"Smidgeon" is the correct term for more than one Smidge.

Why do they fly where the human eye can see them?

Unlike other creatures of fable, the Smidge refused to depart this plane, to leave and go into the West with the Færies. They fear man (as did the rest of their genre, (Feie Spirite) the Sprite family) but more importantly they fear for the safety of the world in the hands of "thems'lot"[1]. It is as if the globe were a rogue Brigatine, crossing stormy seas at the hand of a wreckless and injurious captain.

Their motto;

"Ella Smidga canst dua toute los mæta"

which translates to:

"A Smidge makes all the difference"

is what the Smidgeon truly believe. They have stood by for all time and honestly think they **CAN** make a difference. They defy any obstacle if that obstacle votes in favour of the demon "Elcargo"[2]. In fact, they can be downright naughty at times.

But have a care.

---

1   The human race.
2   Money.

Remember, the Smidgeon (as do the rest of the Feie Spirite), serve the Færie Queen and only want what is best for the world.

This is a story of how the Smidgeon overcame a nasty man in a lesson of hope for us all. But first, let me introduce you to the hero of our story, "Sammo" or "Sammonical Smidge", as he is formally known.

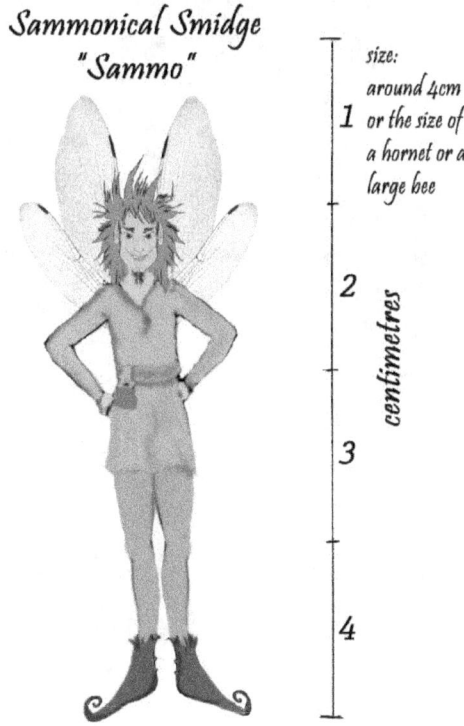

Sammonical Smidge
"Sammo"

size:
around 4cm
or the size of
a hornet or a
large bee

centimetres

1
2
3
4

Sammo lived at Smidgeham, one of four Smidgeon districts. His "haim"[3] was typical of a Smidgeon dwelling, burrowed into the trunk of an old felled Chequer tree. The tiny hamlet was a walled village, an amphitheatric labyrinth of alleys, dead ends and courtyards. At its centre was the village square where, on festival days, the town hall would come alive with seasonal revelry.

To a passerby, the Chequer tree trunk looked like any other tree trunk, but on closer inspection (and with different viewpoint), you could almost make out what those cunning Feie Spirite had craftily

---

camouflaged with Smidge magik. Tiny windows and doors covered by hanging moss and newly grown Chequer leaves.

The haims varied in size, depending upon the number of Smidgeon in the family. Sammo, for instance, had roomy three "beddrums"[4] haim, over two floors.

The family room, which houses the fire, stove, sink and comfy chairs on the ground floor are overlooked by three gallery beddrums on the next floor. As each haim is burrowed into the trunk of the tree, all the windows and entrances are at the front of the dwelling. The walls, ground and ceiling are all wood with intricate carvings over the doorways, window frames, fireplaces and hearths for decoration.

All fixtures, furnishings, plates and cups are made from reclaimed wood and woven grasses off the forest floor. The Smidgeon believe in wasting nothing, long before it became fashionable by "thems'lot"[5]. According to the Smidgeon, "thems'lot" still have not totally got the hang of recycling.

Smidgeon beds and cots are made from woven grasses filled with dandelion feathers to make them soft and then hung from the haim

---

4   Bedroom.
5   Us, humans, the scourge of Smidgeon.

walls and ceiling like hammocks, giving Smidgeon the feeling as if they are flying, even as they sleep.

They do not have bathrooms in the haims, as the Smidgeon wash at the watering pools. This is usually all together, for they are a very social and communal breed. There are several pools, one for washing, one for laundry and another for drinking and cooking. The water for cooking and drinking is carried back to their haims and connected to a pump in the sink.

Nothing is ever wasted. Even the dirty water is reused by watering the land again. Most importantly, Smidgeon share their lives completely. If a new baby is born, clothes and blankets are passed down by the village. This may sound odd but Smidge attire is practical. Practical for flying, practical for working, practical not to draw too much attention to themselves.

Otherwise they may end up like poor old Smitty Smidge, a very vain and audacious Smidge who happened upon a beautiful red piece of velveteen caught on the boundary fence. Smitty stayed up all night sewing and creating a wonderful garment so that he could parade himself to the rest of the Smidgeon at that Twisk's Smeeting.

There he was swishing and whisking about in the dusky light when "snap", along came a swooping gull and ate him whole, never to be

seen again. No-one would have believed such a story unless the Smidgeon had seen it with their own eyes.

Their booties[6] are made from leather, donated by the forest animals. The pelts are stretched and beaten until they are silky soft then they are sewed, curved and buttoned. Their little booties fit snuggly about their shins and fit their feet like a glove except at the toe, where they wind into a long point that curls around and around itself.

The fabric Smidgeon weave their clothes from is an age-old material, passed down by the Fiera, to the Elves, to the Feie Spirite. A fine silk, "Spithrasiol", spun by spiders, is knitted into every kind of garment, blanket or tea cosy imagineable. Depending upon the diet of the spider, the silk can come in a variety of colours ranging from dusky pink to silver grey. Although it looks so very delicate it is harder than chain mail, warmer than angora woollens and more flexible than elastic, leaving room for any Smidge to dive and dart to their heart's content throughout the Smidgeon working day.

On a typical Smidgeon day, a Smidge would rise before the sunrise, so that they can perform the Sun Dance.

---

6   Shoes.

The Sun Dance is a ritual, like a religion, that contains and maintains their faith, spirituality, motivation and health. The Sun Dance consists of five simple movements (a bit like yoga). Stretches that extend both their mind and their wings as they sing the "Sonsonet"[7], leaving the Smidgeon supple and at peace ready to face the day.

Smidgeon have lived side by side with humans for nigh on four millennia. They have watched times change, beliefs come and go and the working week of "thems'lot" change into six working days followed by a day of rest. So to ensure their survival, Smidgeon adapted. However, their months and seasons are the same as the

---

7   An ancient song passed down from the Fiera, sang in the original language of the Gods, in celebration of the creation of the world by the Sun God Ramunil.

Fiera and Elves, which consist of 16 months, each a celebration to the Gods and times of old.

The Smidgeon are the most hardworking of the Feie Spirite, working fully for five days. On the sixth day, they solidly work up until Nonahora[8] then have the rest of the day off. On the seventh day (our Sunday) they cease work for Middameall[9] at midday to spend the rest of the day eating and drinking together, the collective Smidgeon.

Their jobs vary from the highly regarded Magi to Mitters.

The Magi fall into several categories: Magus, Magisters, Quackers, Spechans and Fewmagists.

A Magus is a teacher, a magik maker, magik breaker, upkeeper of the faith and Smidgeon magik lore. In the High Order of Magi, there are those that are rarely seen but who work day in day out to keep the Smidgeon camouflaged. They work beneath the head Magi.

---

8   High Noon.
9   Lunch.

Magisters are the deciders of the lore, makers of the big decisions such as the lessening borders of Smidgeon territory, Smarahaim and such like.

The Quackers are the doctors who dish out their remedies and deal with the day to day good health of the villages. They can most often be seen flying from village to village with their cases under their arm.

The Spechans are the callers at the Smeeting. Spechans take turns to be the Spechan for the night (after nomination by the "'Prim'"[10] on the previous Twisk[11]), to call the notices for the Smeeting. The Prim is the Head of the Order of Spechans and can only be elected by the Head of the Order of the Magi. A Prim will only be replaced after death and seeing as most Smidge tend to live to a ripe old age of 1,000 human years (and often older) those Spechans hoping for elevation can be a long time waiting!

The last under the jurisdiction of the Magi is the Fewamagist who is a newly elected Spechan (only one elected every Fewa[12]). As the most

---

recent member of the Order, the recruit has the job of commencing and closing the Smeeting by banging the Tromme[13].

Comlegs are collectors. Theirs is a vital role, for they fly from village to village collecting post and provisions ensuring the smooth running of the Smidgeon system.

The Byldis are builders. With ever-expanding families, frequently the Smidgeon need alterations on their haims[14], an extra beddrum to be burrowed or a slice borrowed from a neighbour when an adult Smidge moves out and into their own haims.

There is always plenty of building work to be undertaken, just as there will always be a need for Bacas, the bakers. They create and concoct a multitude of delicacies to whet any appetite.

The Fromies are the dairy folk. These cheese makers and creators of all things dairy, make an array of hard and soft cheeses from the milk delivered to them by the Comlegs.

Mitters are messengers who collect the messages for the Smeeting. Theirs is a busy job, chasing scoops and gossip from one village to the next, in search of all the news for the Smeeting that Twisk.

---

13   A large Drum that is banged to commence and finalise a Smeeting.
14   Smidgeon Houses.

The Capari are fishfolk. In Smilad, the Capari fish upon River Breathwater and deliver their wares to their families who in turn sell their catch at the Smidgeham village market. The Capari are highly regarded by the Magi. For these fishfolk are born with the song of the Ocean, a language only fishfolk understand.

This strange language enables them to lull and quieten any monster including the Bugs-of-War (the Werrebuck[15]) as well as the aptitude to coherse fish into their nets.

The Gamas are the keepers of the woods. Gamas make sure the borders are defenced, the magik veils are in tact and fully working, as well as bringing home meatstuffs to the village market.

---

15   A strange looking creature that dwells within the depths of Smarahaim. The Werrebucks are there to protect Smarahaim and the Smidgeon.

Stringans are the musicians and singers. Most Smidge have perfect pitch and love to sing but the Stringans are exceptional, for they have a musical magic in their veins. Stringans can make their voices and instruments emotive to harmonise with every occasion.

It must be pointed out that a Smidge's occupation is destined before they are born.

A member of the Magi will accompany the Quacker on one of the visits to the expectant Smidge. With one hand on the rounded belly the Magi will know instantly what profession the unborn Smidge will become.

Except in the case of the identical twins, Sinas and Smingel Smidge. The Magi got all sorts of signals from them, from Comelegs to Fromies! In the end, the pair of them entered the Order of the Magi, for even as "lumps"[16] they conjured the most mischievous magik, but that is a completely different story!

Bear in mind however that not all Smidge follow in their parents' footsteps, making anything possible and occasionally a Smidge will go against the ruling and choose a different path altogether.

---

16   Unborn Smidge babies.

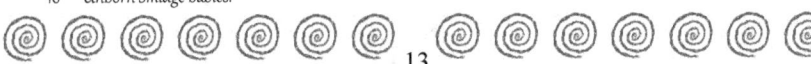

The Smidgeon favourite pastime is eating. So, you can imagine the diversified menu which ranges from "stickleback pie" to "moochi".

Snacabitan and Ealu are both drinks made from the berries of the Chequer tree. Ealu is much less potent and drunk with meals by Smidgeon of adult age. Snacabitan has adder's venom added to it giving it a bite for intoxication. Sranjey is a fruit juice also made from these berries that the children are weaned onto.

The Smidgeon have numerous blends of tea: nettle, strawberry, raspberry, blackberry, blackcurrant, Caithne (which can be either drunk or used as a flavouring in soups, stews and cakes) and Smarantee (which is their favourite) and again is made from the leaves of the Chequer tree.

The Smidgeon are meateaters and eat a variety of meats and fish. A few of their much-loved meals are:

"Stickleback pie" (or stew), "grubs up" (a grub cooked on its back with a layer of pastry laid over it loosely, so its legs point upwards and out through the pastry). "Flearoll" (slithers of flea wrapped in potato and held together by "Casus" (a very mild cheese but quite spongey so it binds and holds). "Woody Pot" is another favourite, a thick steamy stew made from woodlice with big fluffy dumplings.

Smidgeon are extremely keen on snacks, the most favoured is "Gatcas Toasties" (a bit like cheese on toast). "Gatcas" is enormously moreish, a lot like goat's cheese, but much more pongee.

Smidgeon have a terrible sweet tooth and their favourite sweet snack is "Nut Toasties" which consists of a thick slice of bread covered in "moochi"[17], honey and ground hazelnuts.

There are several meal times throughout the Smidgeon day:

"Dawnmeall", is the first meal of the day (just like our breakfast), this is followed a few hours later by a smaller snack-like mealtime called "Searall". Then about an hour later is "Middameall" (lunch). The afternoon is broken into two sections with "Nonamunch", another small snack an hour after lunch and then "Horasnack" a little while later. Refreshments are served before and after the Smeeting. This usually consists of "Fierakaka"[18] and nettle tea or a cup of Ealu on a hot evening.

"Duskemeall" takes place on returning haim after a day's work. This tends to be the biggest meal of the day as the Smidgeon have to go throughout the night without so much as a nibble. But some

---

17   Moochi tastes a lot like chocolate and Smidgeon are addicted to it.
18   Small cakes. Ironically, Fierakaka are fairy cakes so called by "thems'lot" back in the old days when Færies and Man lived hand in hand. The Færies brought King Arthur cakes when he miraculously pulled Excalibur from the stone. Arthur loved them so much he begged the Færie Queen to give his cook the recipe and thenceforth named them Fierakaka "Fairy Cake".

      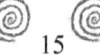

of the younger Smidgeon (mainly Smiguts[19]) tend to wake at "Nihealf"[20] for a "Nihealfin"[21].

The most important event of the Smidgeon day is the Smeeting. This is when you may catch a glimpse of the Smidgeon. At "Twisk"[22], as the sun begins to lower himself to make way for his Lady Moon, so then the Smidgeon hold their Smeeting. The Fewamagist bangs the Tromme,[23] then the Smidgeon do various laps singing the old songs before commencing the "hover",[24] while the Spechan calls the notices of the day (previously delivered by the Mitters).

Although it is a very social gathering, it is mainly adult Smidgeon who attend the Smeeting (Smidgets[25] get far too tired hovering for so long). The Smiguts play around too much and annoy the Grumpties,[26] so usually the just one member of each haim attends.

The Smeeting ends as it begins with the banging of the Tromme, followed by several laps of River Breathwater.

---

19   Teenagers.
20   Midnight.
21   A Midnight Feast.
22   The twilight hour, just before dusk.
23   The big drum to commence the Smeeting.
24   They hover above the river, lake or pond.
25   Babies and Toddlers.
26   Very very old Smidgeon.

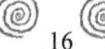

Then it's off to Ye Olde Smidirin, the local tavern, for refreshments and a less formal chat. For Smidgeon love a good old chinwag.

The last and final thing to note is the festivals.

Smidgeon, (as do their cousins, the Pixies), love a sing-song and to dance into the wee hours, so there are countless festivals. All Smidgeon congregate at the hosting village (this alternates each season so every village gets to show off).

The Festivals:

Ånes (our January) is the first feast of the year. A time for new promises and beginnings and it is quite a raucous affair.

Twaïn (usually around February our time) is the Feast of thaw with the symbol of the Phoenix. One Smidge is randomly picked to dance the flight of the Phoenix over the river accompanied by the moon dancers[27].

Theosin (end of February) is the Festival of Starfall. The hosting village decorates every window with a light to celebrate when the Gods fell to earth. At Nihealf they take the candle and meet in the centre of the village where a play of the Starfall is acted out by a group of Smidgeon.

Feøwun (March) is a time for merriment which involves a whole day of festivities including the annual sailing race.

Fifeir (April) is the Festival of rebirth. Kite flying competitions and fireworks at dusky time along with the annual hunt the white rabbit contest.

Saïxon (May) is the quiz festival. A battle of minds takes place from Midday throughout the evening (often until dawn).

Seøfon (June) is the time of drout and the Snacabitan festival. Here the berries of the Chequer are picked, squashed and sampled to make ready the year's supply of Snacabitan with much merriment.

---

27   Fireflies.

Silvatir (July) is the celebration of Mother Earth. Every Smidge of marrying age dances around Smarahaim until midnight. Then one of the Magi, dressed as the werewolf, Banefang, picks out a Moon Queen for the coming year. The singing, dancing and drinking continues into the early hours.

Nigan (August). Another night festival where the Smidgeon meditate until sunset and then sing until the dawn.

Děnthuin (beginning September). The weaving and mending festival where the Smidgeon work all day making and mending clothes until Nonahora when a great feast commences and they parade in their new attire.

Endleøfan (end of September) is the Festival for the Harvest. The Smidgeon work all of this time harvesting ready for the cold winter months. They give thanks to the Sun God at this feast.

Primïn (October) is the Festival of falling leaves. This is the Festival when the Moon Queen is crowned and suitors parade in the hope that she will pick them to be her Sun King. All the Smidgeon vote for the Sun King but in the end, it is the Moon Queen who must decide. Once she makes her choice, the Moon Queen and the Sun King are bound by twine and crowned in leaves. Most of those crowned King and Queen have gone on to marry the following year.

Helodeen (end of October) is the Feast for thanks. A big dance is held in the evening and blessings are given to the Gods for continued love and protection.

Samhalain (beginning November) is the festival of fire. Big fires are lit, the Magi conjure fountains of sparkles and the Smidgeon fly around with the moon dancers.

Bænfife (middle of November) is the festival of gathering. Preparations throughout Baenfife take place for the coming winter. Stocks are checked, doors and windows are fixed or fitted, clothing and furs are taken down from chests at the back of closets and put onto the hammocks in readiness for the frosty nights. The Festival takes place after Nonahora on the day of the New Moon. A Smidge dressed in all white, representing Jack Frost, comes and pinches everyone and then the festivities can begin. If a Smidge has not been pinched, he must find Jack Frost and pinch him before being allowed to "Supp from the cup".

Micælmas (the last day of our December) is the equivalent of our Christmas Day. Smidgeon give each other gifts and sing the old songs. They pass around the "Bïænben"[28] to bind the Smidgeon together and so keep them safe for another year.

---

28   The Binding Cup.

And so this makes up the Smidgeon calendar.

But to hand, we can no longer tarry with this idle banter, there is a story to read. Turn the page and enter the wonderful land of Smidgeon.

Chapter 1

The Smeeting

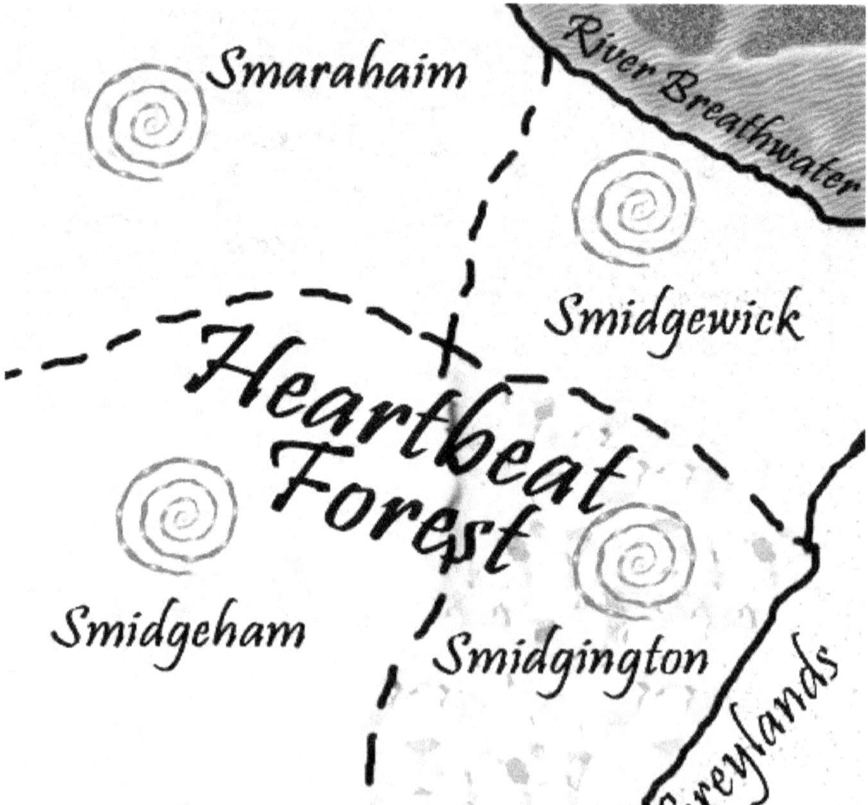

Smarahaim

River Breathwater

Smidgewick

Heartbeat Forest

Smidgeham

Smidgington

Greylands

The ancient land of Smilad diminished daily. Dwindling, it was now split into just four districts: Smidgewick, Smidgington, Smidgeham and Smarahaim.

Smidgewick, was a small settlement nestled on the edge of River Breathwater and home to the families of bakers and fishermen.

Bordering Smidgewick was Smidgington. Smidgington was a petite ringed village whose edges faded with each passing Summer, as the dark and boding Greylands[29] crept slowly closer. Greylands, a looming shadow and a constant threat to those families of the building and weaving crafts who resided there.

Abutting Smidgington and backing onto the age-old woodlands of Heartbeat Forest was Smidgeham. Smidgeham was a tiny hamlet and the quietest of three districts. Largely home to the messengers and collecting kinfolk.

Lastly, but most importantly, was Smarahaim. Deep in the copse, the ancient Chequer Tree sat in the hub of Heartbeat Forest. Smarahaim, as old as the world, stretched her gnarly branches upwards and whispered to the sky.

---

29   Human Housing Estates and built up areas.

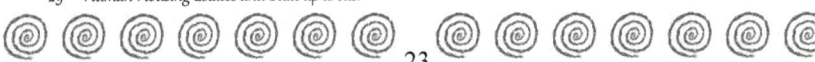

Many many years before, when the Færies first set sail into the West, Smidgeon territories had been boundless. Little by little the Greylands had stolen closer, forcing Smidgeon into their last remaining strongholds.

Smilad was one of those few havens, but threatened daily by the Greylands. Each afternoon, prior to the Smeeting, the Smidgeon elders would deliberate the Greylands and their fears for the ever-growing darkness. Quaffing on jugs of Snacabitan they would discuss and debate.

It was on one of those afternoons that a Smidge called Silus came to join his father, grandfathers and elders in their daily deliberations outside Ye Olde Smidirin at Smidgewick.

Silus, a middle aged Smidge, (about 500 of our years) was the newly elected "Fewamagist"[30] which meant he had the very important role of banging the Tromme to call Smidgeon to the Smeeting.

"Silus." Silures nodded back to his father and the rest of the Smidgeon Elders bowed with him. Silus nodded back to them.

"Tis surely a hot evening Sfarva? Silus said to his Father.

---

30   Master for the Year.

"Aye lad, but there's nothing like a good ol' Smeeting to get the wings back in shape." and the rest of the elders mumbled in agreement with Silures.

"Twill be a good Twisk, but perhaps a wee bit warm for it?" said Silus.

"Aye." Silures said and the elders nodded along with him. "Yet remember, '*there is strain in rain, where no harm's done under sun.*'"everyone chimed.

Silures pointed to a small cluster of clouds on the horizon "...a'sides Boras sends shade."

Silus looked to the horizon and countered "Aye, but Nautil sends rainfall." Silus pointed at the grey shadows under the belly of the cloud.

"Bang the Tromme hasty-like Silus, Smeeting must convene swiftly."

Silures was the "Prim". This meant he opened and closed the Smeeting, as had his father and forefathers done so before him.

The Smeeting was held every night above the River Breathwater. As the sun lowered himself into twilight, covering the waters with deep oranges, reds and pinks against a reedy silhouette, Smidgeon would float above hovering, discussing the issues of the day. The weather, the state of the grass, if the cows were lowing, who was courting, who had been born and how supplies in Smarahaim fared. Most importantly, how far the shadow of Greylands had reached since dawn of that day.

The issue of Greylands had become a torment for the Smidgeon. Already their daily chores had been adjusted to monitor

its progression onto Smilad. The seers predicted that 'the end was nigh' but Silures would hold up his hands and quote the Smidgeon motto "*Ella Smidga canst dua toute los mæta*" ("A Smidge makes all the difference") and peace would return to the Smeeting and Smilad once again.

This Twisk was no different from the rest. Silures hovered in the middle of the ring of Smidgeon and made the first address.

Hail now, hail now, hail now,
Cometh Smidge, Smidge, Smidgeon,
Harpeth, harken, hark now,
Listen Wigeon, Chiff Chaff and Pigeon,
Ring a ring a roseleaf,
Sing a song of serenity,
Widen, widen, wide and flee,
Gap and fly till dusky be.

Silus banged the Tromme again. The Smidgeon flew their laps, winding in and out, singing their songs, until the Tromme banged once more and they all started the hover. Then Silures nodded to Sharkey Smidge who was the "Twisker"[31] so he could start the announcements.

---

31   The Speaker for the Eve.

"Harkety!" yelled Sharkey in a strained and croaky voice, "Shana and Scale Smidge gave birth to their first Smidge at four past dusky. The little Smidgetina is healthy and taken to the Sranjey already!" The throng laughed and nodded in accord with the joyful news. "She'll be named Shalli" Applause erupted above the River.

"Harkety!" Sharkey yelled again (he said this before each new piece of news). Sully and Sable have become affianced with unity vows to be heard over Fewa and binding to commence first dawn of the following Fewa." Again, the congregation "ahhed" and clapped in appreciation.

"Harkety! Poor mother Setty finally lost her battle with croackles[32] and closed the door at six past Twisk last eve. The auld gel was merely Fews away from her Ninohundrid-ninonino[33]. The Moondancers[34] have been notified and "Piradee"[35] takes place ten after dusky on s'morrow." The Smigdeon dipped their heads with sorrow and then flew as if standing upright as they all saluted the Sun, then flew a lap of honour for poor mother Setty.

"Harkety! Ye Olde Snacafest will take place in three score duskies. Smidget's entries for the freewing, backwing, frontwing and

---

32 Old age.
33 999 years old, a much celebrated birthday.
34 Fireflies.
35 The Smidge funeral where the moonflies carry the wrapped body and set fire to it above the river.

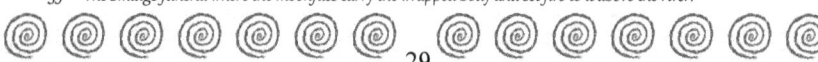

butterfling heats must be in no latesies than dawn after thrice sundowns. Same for the perfect pets prize but all other entries no latesies than dusky eve of the Fest." The crowd became excited and chatted amongst themselves. However the exhilaration was soon stemmed by Sharkey's next and final announcement.

"Harkety! The Greylands edged a record three smidge at "Nonahora".[36]

A groan went through the congregation.

Then one of the Smidge shouted out. He was covered in white-grey dust from his hair to twinkle toes.

"Tis getting wiersa![37] The dry rain pours Sunupsidown[38]!" shouted Sammo as the Smeeting crowd all looked upon him. The assembled Smidgeon started chattering and shouting their fears at the top of their voices just as they had done the night before, and the night before that and ever since the Greylands had inched into Smidgington. As ever, Silures called order to the Smeeting.

---

36   High Noon.
37   Weird and bad.
38   All day (sun up to sun down).

"Harkety! Harkety! Smidgeon! Tis but a way into Smidgington. The seers predict haltings!" yelled Silures but Sammo interjected.

"Aye but the dry rain bears heavy weight upon the soil, the noisy storms scare the wildlife..."

"Harkety! Sammonical Smidge! We thank ye for your daily updates but your pessimistic view of the state of affairs has no bearing at this Smeeting. As we all know "A Smidge makes all the difference!" said Silures quoting the Smidgeon motto and with this he nodded to his son Silus who banged the Tromme to call the end of the Smeeting. With the last bang of the Tromme resounding over the water, the Smidgeon flew their last lap whilst singing the final song of the evening.

"Nightee, nightee, cease the flightee,
Wither whispee wish for snooze;
Byesie, byesie, till morrow comesie,
Bringan sun and joyful news;
Fare-thee, fare-thee, well and wishty,
Wishty goodness for sandy sleep;
Carefree, carefree, happy all be,
Safe and sound without a peep."

And then off they flew back to their homes in Smidgewick, Smidgington, Smidgeham and Smarahaim before it became too dusky to fly.

Chapter 2

The Twins

Sammo flew back to Smidgeham in a foul mood. He mumbled all the way home about the dry rain and how Silures never paid him any mind. Sammo's wife Selina had made him his favourite dish, stickleback pie, but even this could not lift his mood. He ate in silence, supping at his jug of Ealu in between shoveling in hefty mouthfuls of pie.

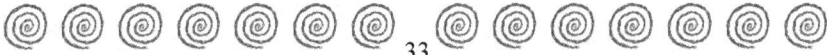

"Good Smeeting Sluf?" Selina asked cheerily.

"No Sluf, twas same as ever! Silures denying the Greylands draw closer, even though 1 stood before him covered in the dry rain!" barked Sammo.

"Oh dear! Have more pie Sluf?" Sammo nodded as Selina scooped more of the pie onto his plate.[39]

Sammo's mood lifted with each spoonful. He almost managed to return a smile back to his wife on his third helping of pie. Sammo was always like this after each Smeeting because he felt as if he was the only Smidge who had any true concern for the Greylands. Sammo was a "Comleg", a collector. He would fly between the four districts collecting news, supplies and mail. His daily routine had been adjusted to take in Greylands at Nonahora when he would measure the shadows. Most days this was nigh on impossible due to the dry rain. Sheets and sheets of white-grey dust would fly into his eyes while the noise of the storm would almost deafen him. Poor Sammo had cuts and bruises all over him where he had flown into a branch or misjudged a landmark because he could not see.

---

39   The Smidge appetite is bottomless, so there is always hot food on the stove for if they are not flying or sleeping they are eating.

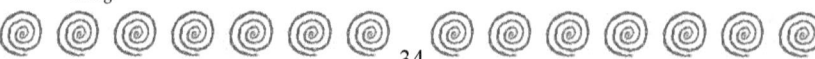

Today had been no exception, he had flown into a tornado of dry-rain and clamour. The dust got into his eyes and mouth and he flew blindly until he was swished into the side of Ealdo the Oak Tree by one of the cow's tails. Sammo's arms were covered in grazes and he had a nasty bruise on his head which Selina had not noticed when he first arrived home because the dust covered him from head to twinkle toe giving him a somewhat ghostly appearance. Thankfully, his injuries did not stop him from stuffing large quantities of pie into his mouth and finally, with a full belly he sat back in the chair and looked softly at his wife.

"I'm sorry Sluf." he said taking her palm and kissing it.

"S'alright Sluf, you're always a mizzog after Smeetings. Twas the pie good?" she said changing the conversation away from the Smeeting.

"Pie, as always, was magnifico!" he said grabbing her around her waist and pulling her onto his lap. Selina screamed and laughed pretending that she did not want his dust to get on her clean wings.

"Go bathe yerself Sammonical Smidge!" she harped in feigned annoyance. "Your Smidgets want their dusky kiss."

With this reminder Sammo flew off to the Eallpool[40] to rub himself clean. But my, oh my, how his arm and head hurt. Once he was scrubbed nice and clean, he returned to their lodge where Selina had built up the fire and was now sitting in the rocking chair knitting. Sammo went into the Smidgets' beddrum and quietly looked at his little Smidgets sleeping soundly. He placed a gentle kiss on each of Samus' and Sashsi's forehead but before he had

---

40   The communal pool where all the Smidge bathed.

moved from the room the two Smidgets were awake and squealing for their father to read them their favourite book. Sammo picked up the book from the little wooden table and sat at the foot of their hammocks.

"Scancalang the Great and the curse of the Snapdragon"

Both the Smidgets squeaked with glee and clapped. Their little Smidget eyes, wide with excitement, as Sammo read from the tales

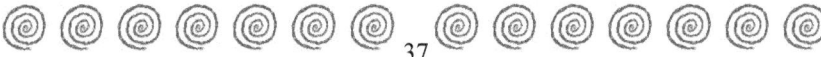

of the famous Smidge, Scancalang and his adventures in the days of the Færie Queen.

Despite the story being read time and time again, Sashsi was too excited to sleep. She had been put into the top class in her lessons and she was jumping up and down on the hammock as she told Sammo her good news. Being in the top class meant learning the lores of the Magi which included languages. Sashsi was brimming over at the thought of learning the language of "thems'lot". She was babbling so much that Selina came in to calm her down, blaming Sammo for waking the wee ones.

She was not crabby long, for she noticed poor Sammo's bruise and grazes. Selina tucked the Smidgets back into their hammocks and then made a fuss of poor Sammo. She bathed his arm with witch hazel and rubbed fresh ash softly onto his bruised head covering it with a slither of dandelion leaf to be worn until the morning. Then she kissed his face all over (except where the bruise was) and made him some hot milk with hazelnut and moochi (which tasted just like hot chocolate) and sat him by the fire.

"Another bad day, Sluf?" she asked as she continued her knitting.

"'Aye Sluf, tis getting harder. The dry rain falls hard and the storm bellows like a hungry monster."

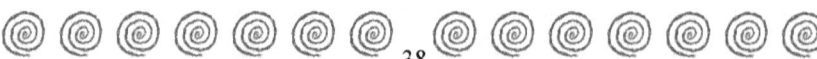

"Aye, but was good news about Sashsi, no?"

"Aye twas, but why do they makes 'ems learn "Mansprek" though Sluf?"

"Tis part of her Magi training. And cos she's clever. Mind, can't say as she got it from your side of the family tree!" Selina said laughing and rocking at the same time as knitting.

Sammo joined her in laughing. It was their joke, Selina always goaded Sammo that the brains came from her side of the family tree.

"So when does she start learning it?" he asked.

"On the morro, she moves into the top class straight away."

"Cripes! She must have your brains." and they both laughed again so hard that Selina had to stop knitting.

"Watcha knitting?" Sammo asked.

"Booties." Selina replied.

"Who for?" he asked rocking back and forth subconsciously imitating Selina's rocking motion.

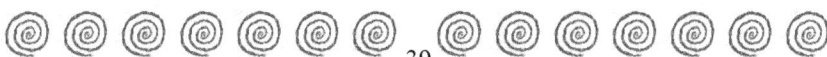

"Sabine and Sabina." Selina said calmly.

"Who are Sabine and Sabina?" asked Sammo.

"The twins." she replied.

"Who's twins?" Sammo asked.

"Our twins." she continued just as calmly.

"We don't have twins?" said Sammo quizzically.

"Not yet but we will by the end of this Fewa." she replied.

Sammo's eyes widened as he looked at Selina's belly. He laughed and whooped and ran to kiss her.

"And there's me thinking that you'd just had too much pie!" he shouted as he cuddled her.

"Hush Sammo, you'll wake the Smidgets again!" she chided him with a wide smile on her face.

"How long have you known?" enquired Sammo.

"A wee while but I didn't want to worry you till I was sure. The Quacker has given me the timings but I wanted to surprise you."

"Well Sluf, you've certainly done that!" Sammo said smiling. But his smile did not last for long before he became sombre again.

"What is it Sluf?" Selina was worried.

"It's the Greylands. They grow nearer and we'll have two more Smidgets to feed and worry for. What sort of land is this to bring Smidgeon into?" he shook his head.

"Worry not Sluf. Smidgeon have always coped with the changing landscape. All bodes well. The Quacker told me so, 'sides, I bumped into Smelton of the Magi and he insisted on revelating the lumps. He's convinced I'm holding Stringans.". Selina grinned.

"Stringans! What use are they! Singing wonders!" Sammo humpfed.

"They are very well regarded by the Magus and Magisters because they hold the Smeeting together with their voices."

"Mmm, well it wonna stop the Greylands from growing though will it?" Sammo chided.

Selina sensed Sammo's fears. She stopped knitting and stood behind him, rubbed his shoulders and told him not to worry but still Sammo could not shake off the feeling of impending doom.

They retired to bed in the hope Sammo would wake in a better frame of mind.

Chapter 3

The Gateway

Sammo woke at the usual time, two breaths before Sunrise. He stretched his whole body and then rubbed his blue eyes. Selina was already up, preparing the Smidgets for the Sun Dance.

Today would be a fine day, the mist clung low to the ground and the cattle stood as if floating upon the sea of mist. It would be a scorcher Sammo thought and this cheered him up.

They commenced the Sun Dance as the sun's rays exploded onto the land, warming their faces with golden kisses. They stretched and pulled until the cockerel crowed a third time, then it was time for "Dawnmeal", the first meal of the day. Nut toasties covered with honey or moochi for the Smidgets and lashings of hot nettle tea.

"What day today S'farva?" asked Samus.

"'Today will be a scorcher, Samus my boy." replied Sammo.

"What did ye do to ye head S'farva?" asked Sashsi.

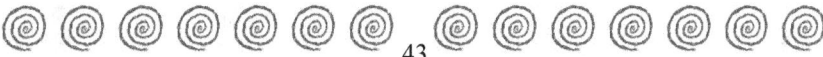

"Ooh that reminds me" interjected Selina and she took a damp cloth to Sammo's bruised head and wiped the dandelion leaf so it came off in one piece leaving only a faint yellow bruise underneath it.

"I banged into a tree Sashsi. That mooty[41] dry rain blinded and choked me so it did. Still could have been wiersa!" Sammo said chuckling.

"Does the rain get into your eyes then S'farva?" asked Samus.

"Aye my lad. Sometimes tis impossible to see my hand in front of my face! Looksey at my arm." said Sammo as both the Smidgets gasped "I reckon luck was on my side."

"Poor DaDa." said Sashsi as both Smidgets slipped down from the table, kissed their parents and ran to ready themselves for school.

"Ye should be more careful Sammo." said Selina "Ye should have a word at the Smeeting tonight."

"Some chance of being heard Sluf! See I'm annoyed again just thinking about it." and with that he skulked off to ready himself for a day of collecting.

---

41   Nasty.

Selina took the Smidgets to the Bridan[42] where the Blackbird would take all the Smidgets of Smidgeham to their lessons in the schoolhouse at Smarahaim. Sashsi was uncontrollably excited, for today she would begin lessons in High Class which meant learning "Mansprek"[43]. This Fewa they would start with Anglii (English), then proceed onto Latium (Latin), Greca (Greek) and finally Samskri (Sanskrit) and Sumbulon (hieroglyphics). As a lump, Selina had been told that Sashsi would enter the Magus and go on to train as a Magi, the highest honour for any Smidge.

Selina waved goodbye as the blackbird flew off in the direction of Smarahaim. She then set about her chores.

Meanwhile, Sammo had zipped to and fro, collecting the mail and messages. As he had made good time, he thought he would pass by the Greylands to check on the storm. As he had predicted, the day was turning into a scorcher. It was usual on every sixth and seventh day the storms would subside and as today was the sixth day, all was calm as Sammo flew up to the boundary. Calm that is except for a new shadow. A large and many coloured gateway had been erected on the line of the border. Sammo saw this as no less than

---

42   Bus Stop.
43   The language of humans.

"thems'lot's" way of insulting Smilad in the utmost (or as he would put it "twas 'streemly eirrie of "thems'lot"").

Sammo was so incensed that he almost dropped the provisions he had collected from the Bacas[44] because he zoomed so quickly back to Smarahaim. Once there he rapidly delivered the messages, mail and provisions to proceed in seeking out Silures who was nowhere to be found.

This left Sammo in an even "wiersa" mood and poor Selina had to feed him lashings of freshly cooked fish soup, nutty bread and moochi before she managed to get even a windy smile from his lips.

The Smidgets arrived home early, full of the joys of their lessons especially Sashsi who was speaking in a funny language.

"Anglii" she said, but to Sammo, Selina and Samus it sounded like goobledegook. Needless to say, Sashsi was brimming over with exhilaration. Poor Sammo seemed in a daze, so Selina suggested he fly the Smidgets down to the Market at Smidgewick to collect some shopping for their lunch and dinner on the morrow.

On Selina's instructions, the three of them whizzed down to Smidgewick.

---

44   The Bakers.

Sashsi was in charge of the list:

four breast of woodlice
a quarter grub
half a flea

The shopping nearly filled the basket to the top. Samus had begged to be in charge of holding the basket but it was almost as big as him and way too heavy making him weave back and forth across the shop. Both Sashsi and Sammo giggled at the sight of the little Smidget whose face was bright red from having too much weight to carry for such a wee Smidget. Sammo took the basket from Samus who secretly breathed a sigh of relief.

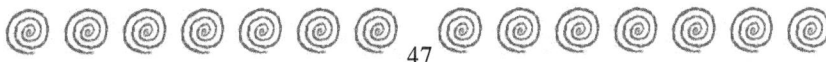

By then the sun was high and they were all very thirsty, so Sammo took them to Ye Old Smidirin. Here they sat and had a drink on the riverbank while watching the "tiddlers" weaving around in the water.

It was nearly Nonahora so Sammo decided to fly them all back passed the borders so the Smidgets could play their usual game of "Comeleg Searchy". For this game, they would collect unusual objects for their scrap books. Then these objects would be entered

into the Comeleg Searchy Competition at Snacafest for a grand prize of a trip to the Moochimaker with lots of free jars of moochi thrown in.

When the search was over, the three of them sat basking in the afternoon glow, watching the shadows lengthen, the sky grew deeper blue with every swish of the cow's tail. There was not a cloud to be seen for miles.

"Them's cows are mad." Sammo unconsciously said aloud.

"But why DaDa?" asked Sashsi.

"Cos there's no Brownies left to talk and guides 'em." he replied.

"But where did the Brownies go DaDa?" she asked.

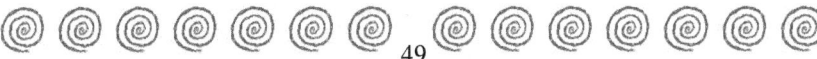

"The Brownies went with the Færie Queen, Sashsi. A handful stayed behindes, but t'wernt long before "thems'lot" got rid of those an' all." Sammo said sadly shaking his head.

"But what did the Brownies do DaDa?" asked Samus.

"Well Samus, the Brownies are the herdsfolk. They maintained the herd, fields and lands. Brownies speak Boradine y'see, the language of herd animals, so tis no wonder that the cows have all gone "doolally-tat" with only themselves for company or a passing Elk to talk to. Let me tell yous, thems Elks are not big on conversations. The Brownies would keep the peace and order and bring the land to life with their earth magic. For the herds this was the meaning of life. All's been lost without the Brown folk. You should pity those poor mad cows for they can see no beauty without the Brownie." Sammo explained with tears in his eyes.

"Because "thems'lot" will rid 'emselves of anything they fears or dunnat understand. Mind ye in the case of these Greylands tis anything that stands in the way." Sammo ushered both the Smidgets away for he could feel himself getting angry again.

"What's that DaDa?" asked Samus flying to the new gateway.

Bruff Estates
LUXURY
3 and 4 bedroom homes
brought to you
by
Bruff Estates
For Sale

"Have a care Samus!" shouted Sammo after the little Smidget.

He flew and caught hold of Samus before he could reach the gateway ushering them both back haim but Sashsi had fallen behind and was hovering in front of the gateway looking intently at the colours.

"Sashsi! Come away, we must head for haim." Sammo yelled.

"Ooh DaDa this dunnat look good. You were right about it beings wiersa!" she told him.

"Whatdeyemean?" he asked flying over to her.

"Wells, thems colours as you mentions, thems be words, "Mansprek", and it says: 'For Sale. Luxury three and four bedroom homes brought to you by Bruff Estates, en...erm...enque...erm...enquire within" that's what it says!" Sashsi beamed proudly.

"Well what's 'Sluxury'?" asked Sammo.

Dunno DaDa, I can look it up in the words book on the morrow?"

"Aye Petsie, me finks it dunnat sounds good. "Homes" must mean haims? That could mean "thems'lot" moving in as neighbourly. Cripes we cannut have it!"

In a panic, Sammo gathered up the Smidgets and flew home at top speed. He breathlessly relayed their findings from the sign to Selina before shooting off without tea and almost taking the basket of food with him but for Selina chasing after him.

"Sammo!" she cried "Pray calm down! You'll drive Silures doolally-tat if you dunnat get with its!"

"Aye." he nodded frantically but whizzed off nonetheless.

The Smeeting did not convene immediately so Sammo had another half of Ealu to calm his nerves. As he sat in the dwindling sunlight, he felt sure Silures would have to listen to him today.

Chapter 4

Sashsi and the Goggles

Sammo slammed the door behind him making Selina jump up from her rocking chair with a start.

"Sammonical! What in the Færie Queen?" she chided him as Sammo slumped down into a dining chair, his head in his hands, shaking it from side to side.

"He wonnat listen! He shot me down in flames again Sluf!" Sammo said desperately. Selina put her arms around him. "Why wonna he listen to me? I mean the Gateway, all he needed to do was come and sees for himself!" Sammo looked into Selina's eyes.

She could see his distress. "I know Sluf, but what else can ye do?"

"A Smidge makes all the difference! I dunna think so, cos by the end of this Fewa there'll be no Smidgeon left if he carries on ignoring my warnings! It's time for action not sitting on the border."

"Oh dear" exclaimed Selina not knowing what to do.

Then two little pairs of eyes appeared at the end of the table. A wide-eyed, Sashsi and Samus looked up blinking at their father. Sammo and Selina looked at the pair of wee ones and then at each other. Then Sashsi lead Samus by the hand and stood in front of Sammo.

"DaDa dunnat be noisy, the lumps wannot likesit." Sashsi whispered and Samus nodded in agreement. "We made a present." She and Samus handed their father a bundle of leather.

"Put it ons DaDa!" yelped Samus eagerly.

"We've been working hard all evening to get it right." said Sashsi.

Sammo pulled on the leather straps forcing down the hat that the Smidgets had made. Sashsi nipped behind Sammo, flipped down a flap and tied a few knots. She then produced a soft thin scarf that she tied around Sammo's nose and mouth.

"Can ye breathe still DaDa?" she asked peering closely through the holes of the hat to look into his eyes. Sammo nodded and Sashsi grinned.

"Perfectomundo!" she beamed. "See yourself in the looking glass DaDa!"

Selina held her hand over her mouth to suppress her amusement. Sammo looked at himself in the looking glass and burst out laughing. Suddenly he could not be angry any more. The hat was made of leather and sat firmly on his head, forcing his thick wirey red hair to spray out from under it. A flap of leather hung down over his forehead, this had two holes. Fixed into the holes were pieces of glass that made Sammo's eyes look enlarged like saucers. The flap was fastened by a knot and this is why Sashsi had tied flaps behind his head for it kept the flap fastened to his face enabling him to see through the glass.

He was a sight to behold. He looked like a bug and with the soft brown scarf about his nose and mouth he was set to fly the skies over the Greylands.

"Thank ye Smidgets!" he grinned from behind his mask.

"We dunnat wantcha to get hurtsied any mores DaDa." said Sashsi holding onto Sammo's legs. Samus joined in, screwing up his nose to show two missing front teeth.

"I'll be just fine and dandy with this contrapt-sheeun." he nodded.

Selina still laughing, came and cuddled her little ones. She nuzzled them and chivvied them away to their room. As Selina scootered them back to bed, Sashsi called out.

"Ooh DaDa, I forgets to tell yees, 'Luxury' means very upper noodle haims." She beamed again, proud to be able to impart some of her new-found knowledge.

"Thank ye Petsie, sleep sandysound, till the morrow."

With that, Selina put both the Smidgets to bed. Sammo looked at himself and laughed. Selina came and helped him out of the contraption and they both chortled some more. They agreed how

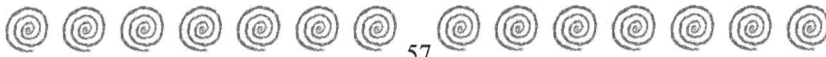

lucky they were to have two such loving Smidgets and then they retired for the evening.

Sammo dreamt of Brownies dancing around the Greylands, but in his dream, there was no shadow. The cows were singing and swaying as the Færie Queen came and gave him a crown made from a bluebell. He woke startled but happy. Everything was alright, he convinced himself, until he realised it had been but a dream and so his doldrums returned.

On the sixth day, work was limited to the hours before Nonahora, but on the seventh day work finished at midday enabling the Smidgeon to eat at Ye Olde Smidirin as a family. Everyone rushed around in the morning, to ensure all chores and jobs had been completed, leaving the afternoon relaxed and worry-free.

Sammo felt confused. He was in a happy mood because of his wonderful dream but this conflicted with his emotional sensation of doom. He could not escape the reality of the Greylands. He tried to console himself by rushing around the villages collecting. At the end of his rounds he nipped back home and picked up the Smidgets for a wee treat of Comleg searchy.

The Snacafest was drawing closer and he knew his Smidgets wanted to put in a good entry. Yet again their search took them close to the border where the new Gateway loomed high above.

However, today there was something different about the Gateway. There were more colours and some new signs had been added covering over some of the other signs. Sammo, Samus and Sashsi all hovered looking up at it. Sammo looked to Sashsi who was tilting her head to one side. Then with wide eyes she looked at her father and cried.

"Oh no DaDa! "thems'lot" are looking to builds more noodlehaims right here in Smigdington!"

Sammo thought that his head was going to explode when two of "thems'lot" (menfolk) appeared from out of a hole in a wall and headed straight towards them. Sammo grabbed the Smidgets and flew to the top of the Gateway, landing on it with a jolt.

Sammo, Sashi and Samus looked down as the two menfolk came even closer towards them. They were speaking the Mansprek. The three Smidgeon watched on, as two middle aged portly looking gentlemen (for humans that is) pointed and shook heads as they conversed.

"Well Bruff, this is green belt. I couldn't possibly sign off planning permission without questions being asked." said the shorter and marginally thinner of the two men.

"Very well Crossford, how much this time?" replied the stout, ruddy cheeked gentleman as he ran his fat fingers through what was left of his mop of thinning red hair.

"Well, erm... well, I'd be taking much more of risk this time... believe you me, questions were asked before and I had to dodge a lot of bullets on the last application I put through for you Bruff..."

"How much Monty?" asked Bruff, his cheeks reddening further.

"...it would take a lot of explaining and greasing of individual palms on this occasion..." Monty implored.

"Goddamit Monty, I get the message, name your price!" Bruff shouted his face turning a darker shade of scarlet.

"...it...it...it's not I don't want to help... but my wife, I have children...both Phoebe and Giles attend good schools ... I'd hate to ruin their lives as well as my own..."

"Monty!" Bruff yelled in desperation.

Monty feigned shock but secretly was mentally counting the gold shekels he intended to extract from Bruff's open offer.

"You get a ten per cent slice of the overall cake which is more than generous. On the figures alone from the last sales you'll be able to put those blasted brats of yours into a school on the moon! I suggest a one-off payment of say "Five hundred kay. Enough for you to pay off your Council worms and take Diana on a nice holiday as the application goes through."

"mmmm ... five hundred thousand pounds is not a lot of money considering what the land is worth..." tried Monty.

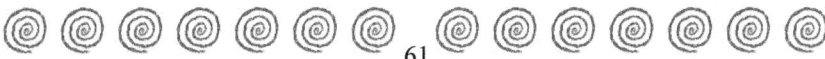

"Don't try it with me Monty! You were hopeless at bartering back at school. Leave the deals to Big Bruffer! Now will you shake on it?" pressed Bruff.

'mmmm...., will it be in cash?"

"Of course it's in ruddy cash man, how on earth can I lose five hundred grand, if I have to write a cheque out for it! It'd be as good putting an advertisement in the Swale Gazette 'local Councillor accepts £500k bribe for top quality turf!'" Bruff groaned in desperation.

Finally, Monty extended his right hand and they shook on their corruption.

"I can't believe that this time next year this landscape will be full of new homes!" said Monty.

"Yes, but more importantly, new Bruff Homes!" and the pair laughed a deep sickly laugh that only those without any soul can muster.

Sashsi looked to Sammo. She had understood most of their conversation and the bits she had not heard or understood she had worked out for herself.

"Oh DaDa!" she whispered, tears welling up in her eyes. "We's for the chop, like in the book about 'Scancalang and the Woodsmen'". All three of them gulped.

"Pray Sashsi." Sammo uttered "What did it all mean?"

"Oh DaDa, "thems'lot" are building haims! Lots and lots of haims, so not one Smidge will be left. The nasty men talked about Elcargo so musts be weirsa than even you thinks DaDa!" Sashsi's bottom lip began to tremble and Samus started to cry because his sister was upset. Sammo scooped them both up and headed off down to Smidgeham to Ye Old Smidirin where Selina was meeting them. She had ordered their food so it would be ready for them, but looked on in disbelief as her two little Smidgets stood sobbing hysterically over what they had seen. Sammo tried to calm them and Selina scolded him for taking them back to the Greylands but Sashsi defended her father.

"We asked DaDa to take us S'muvva!" she blurted out in between floods of tears "Poor DaDa has been right all along!" she wailed.

It was not very long before the rest of the Smidgeon congregated into the Tavern and wondered on all the fuss. The word went around and soon all hell was let loose the moment Silures walked in with his wife and children.

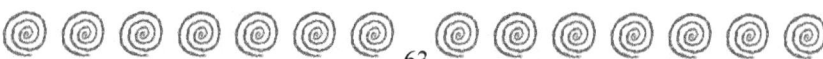

"Hear ye this Silures!" shouted one of the Elders to him.

"Hear I what old Shonka?" answered Silures in his usual superior tone.

"Sammo was right all alongs about Greylands!"

Silures rolled his eyes and smiled condescingly. "What nonsense have you been spreading now Sammo?" Silures patronised Sammo. Sammo stood there dispirited, he knew Silures would not believe him. The Tavern was hushed and all eyes fell upon Sammo who began to tell the story again but before he had got past the news of the new Gateway, Sashsi barged in front of him and screamed.

"Ye never listen to my Sfarva, but I heards "them'slot" talking with my own lugholes and I knows what they says. I read the signs and "them'slot" are moving in neighbourly, but weirsa than neighbourly, "thems'lot" are taking over, Smidgington, Smidgham, and Smidgewick are for the chops!" and she burst into tears again and ran into her mother's arms.

The Smidgeon erupted. Then an ancient voice boomed and resounded throughout the throng. A very old Smidge, who was bent over almost double, walked staff in hand into the centre of the room as a silent crowd looked on at the oldest Smidge any had seen.

Long white strands of hair hung loosely about his wrinkled face and his dark piercing eyes shone out behind his silvery skin as he looked around the room.

"Not many of ye have set eyes upon us for nigh on hundri' Fews." said the old Smidge. "S'pose you must have thought me burnt by the Moondancers be nigh?" he continued but no-one dared utter a word. "Well I'm still here!" he chuckled with a toothless grin. The throng laughed a guarded laugh along with him.

This Smidge was Sinas. Head of the Magi. The most powerful of all the Smidgeon. All knowing was he, for he was a maker and breaker of magik.

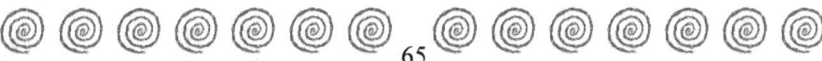

"Where is Sammonical Smidge?" he asked but Silures interfered.

"There is no reason to trouble yourself with the ramblings of a fool, my Lord." Silures trivialised.

"Harkety!" yelled Sinas "Who put ye in charge?" Sinas held Silures in his stare, his lips pursed ready to release a tirade. Silures quaked in his twinkle boots.

"You did your Grace." Silures replied bowing his head but not daring to take his eyes from Sinas.

"Well just you remember that tyrstups[45]! Sinas glared at him. "Now, where is Sammo?"

Poor Sammo was shaking in his boots. Little Sashsi grabbed Sammo's hand and refused to let go, frowning at him when he tried to remove his hand from her grasp. The pair of them edged slowly forward to stand before the old master.

"Well well well. What have we here?" Sinas chuckled at the sight of Sashsi. "Sashsi Smidge. I know ALL about you little Smidget." Sashsi looked back at Sinas with her big brown eyes.

---

45 Upstart.

"Now there's no reason for the Suneall[46] to be disturbed. Ye best get munching whiles Sammo, Sashsi and I takes a wee flip out to this 'ere Gateway". He winked at Sammo and Sashsi then manoeved them both out of the door, leaving the Tavern in a stunned silence.

---

46   Sunset meal.

Chapter 5

Dung Bombs

Sinas asked Sammo to show him the whereabouts of the Gateway. The day was moving along and so the shadows were almost touching the borders of Smidgington. As Sinas saw this, he sighed and shook his head.

As they reached the Gateway way Sinas hovered looking at it. "Aye, she was right. Sashsi, you've the making of a great and powerful Magi. Sammo, you should be very proud." Sinas said with a warm smile for Sashsi who was beaming up at her father.

"Right then back for Suneall!" shouted Sinas speeding off, leaving the two of them behind. They flew after him surprised how agile the old master was, for he beat them easily back to the Tavern by at least three breaths.

Sammo and Sashsi were fairly out of breath by the time they reached Ye Old Smidirin. Sinas turned to Sammo and shook his hand, ruffled Sashsi's dark curly hair and winked again. Then shouting at the top of his voice, he flew off again. "...be seeing ye later Sammo!"

The noise in the Tavern was deafening when Sammo and Sashsi returned. Selina beckoned them to a table in a corner away from the main crowd, where their parents, grandparents, grantyparents and old grumpties sat about discussing the events of the day. Luckily Sammo and Sashsi's arrival went unnoticed, as is usually the case when there is food on the table.

Nothing more was said about the happenings with Sinas, nor about the Greylands. Even at the Smeeting that Twisk nothing was mentioned and Sammo felt too embarrassed to stand up again to battle with Silures who equally was taking a backseat role after his dusting down by Sinas.

Twisk turned dusky and all the Smidgeon were back in their "haims" preparing for bed and a new day. Well, all that is except Silures, Sharkey, Stoutnose and Shayle.

Silures had called an urgent S'late Smeeting. These meetings happened very rarely and mostly only in the "weirsa" circumstances. Silures decreed that on Sinas' appearance events had changed and this was utmostly 'weirsa".

The four of them practically wore out the floor of the Smarahaim Lorechamber walking to and fro, trying to reach a solution. They had no idea what should be done but it was now very apparent that "thems'lot" were planning to be more than "neighbourly" and that it was time for the Smidgeon to act. On and on they talked into the wee hours till it was almost Nihealf[47]. Still Silures had no answer.

"There's nothing that can be done." Silures said sitting on the Magister's throne with his head in his hands.

As the owls hooted the calling[48] of Nihealf, an unexpected visitor joined the S'late Smeeting.

"I thought I may finde ye hearaslike." said Sinas wryly.

"Your Grace!" Silures jumped up to greet the most ancient of all the elders. "We canst make amends." Silures began to rant. Sinas put

---

47 Midnight.
48 Three "whoots" followed by one "whoohoo" followed by a further three "whoo whoo whoohoohoos".

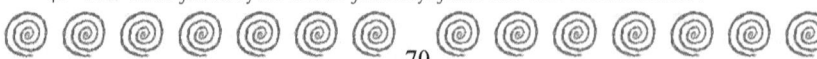

his hand on Silures' shoulder to calm him as he addressed all four of them.

"Trouble ye no longer, "thems'lot" be a lore of their own. A lore above Smidgefolk. We must now seek a higher hand."

"He's talking in riddles." Sharkey whisperered to Shayle.

"...riddles say ye Sharklefrond" Sinas scowled at Sharkey who cowered at his faux pas (for Sinas' ears still had the clarity of a bat) "...riddles to those without the nous! Hear this! At the morrow's Twisk, on the call of the Smeeting the Harkety shall go out for Greylands. Silures you must ask the Smidgeon to gather the dung of the herds, the Magi will set about to make the potions and we will bombard "thems'lot" with poisons."

The four Elders nodded in approval and Sinas walked across the Lorechamber. As he reached the large wooden doors, he turned around and said "it'll keep em at bay for a while till my letters have reached the Isle." Then he chuckled to himself and disappeared.

Silures and Sharkey looked at each other blankly and shrugged. There was much work to be done. The Smidgeon would need to work flat out throughout that next day and night collecting dung, preparing to keep "thems'lot" at bay.

Sammo had the dream again, but this time it was really sinister.

The Færie Queen looked darkly upon him. She was angry so he ran away but he was running in mud so he could barely lift his legs. He woke up with a start. His heart was in his mouth and he was gasping for breath. Selina was looking down at him her face filled with worry.

"Sluf?" she asked.

"Just a dream Sluf." Sammo whispered, relieved that it really was only a dream. "Just a dream." The pair of them snuggled up together and slept until the first crow of the new dawn.

Sammo's collecting rounds went quickly and soon it was time to check on the Greylands. As it was the first day of a new week, the dry rain would be falling hard, Sammo donned his new headwear.

At first, he found it hard getting used to the glasses. Everything was magnified, so most things appeared either really close, or in the case of the cows, they appeared to be the size of monsters.

"Cripes!" Sammo gulped as he flew out of Smidgington passing by the herd "dunnat know whats thems Bovies[49] have been eating to makes'em grow so big overnight."

He promptly he took off the headgear to check on his surroundings and breathed a sigh of relief.

"Bejumblings, me finx for a breath that me Sluf had put ye olde Snacabitan in my moochi!" he laughed heartily to himself.

As predicted, the dry rain poured down hard and the thunder boomed, but surprisingly the headwear that Sashsi and Samus had made for their father proved to be a great success. The leather straps held his ears flat and stopped some of the noise. The dry rain[50] found it difficult to cling to the glass and the scarf helped Sammo breathe.

His new headgear made what was usually a harrowing experience almost enjoyable. Well almost and as no other developments had occurred since the previous day, Sammo was lulled into a cheery mood.

As he had time on his hands, Sammo popped into Ye Old Smidirin and shared a mug of Ealu along with the rest of his and Selina's

---

49 Cows.
50 Dust.

family, who were playing "Plegadabord[51]" whilst telling the "auld storyes".

Plegadabord

Most of the stories were very tall tales but it left Sammo feeling quite jolly. The Trommes called them all to the Smeeting and today Sammo was happy to just hover quietly and enjoy the Smeeting, as

---

51 A table game involving as many players that you wish but at least 2. The more players the harder the game is. The table is the board. A player has a home (like Ludo) and must make it through the board rolling an octagonal dice (if you get 8 you roll again). It's a bit like snakes and ladders as you have to get to the middle. The last one to get there wins the game which is typical of Smidgeon who always seem to do things backwards.

he had been able to in years gone by. Unfortunately, this was not going to be the case tonight.

After the introductions and most of the announcements, Silures took the final "Harkety!"

"Harkety!" he called and all fell silent "I call Sammonical Smidge to the circle".

Poor Sammo groaned "What now?!" he thought to himself as he flew from the back of the group to the front of the congregation. Everyone was looking at him and Sammo felt a tad embarrassed.

"Sammo!" cried Silures and Sammo nodded. "Hear ye all this! Sammonical Smidge has been in charge of the overseeing of the Greylands. He has done a marvellous job."

The crowd cheered while Sammo thought suspiciously to himself *"what's this old fool after?"*

"It has been decreed that on Sammo's findings, we can no longer sit by and let "thems'lot" trample and sully Smidgeon territory. We must make a stand!" The congregation cheered in agreement.

"Sammo?" Silures said turning to poor Sammo (who, by the way, was still wondering what Silures had up his sleeve and what on

earth it had to do with him). "In ye capacity as Comeleg and may I say one of the best Comeleggies we've ever had." Silures added obsequeciescly "Ye have been given the historical task of heading the Dung Comeleggie team." Silures beamed at Sammo who just stared back at him blankly.

Sammo was young in terms of Smidgeon, but even as young as he was, he had heard tales of the Dung Comeleggies of the Battle of 1856. Albeit a responsible task, it was a dirty job and Sammo could not help thinking that Silures was finally getting his revenge upon him.

"Will ye take the task young Sammo?" Silures asked.

Sammo knew he could not say "no". He nodded his agreement. The crowd clapped and Silures asked for Comeleggies and any other volunteers to report to Sammo after the Smeeting. Collecting would begin directly after Sun Dance, all day until enough ammunition had been collected for the Magi in order for them to make their potions.

Sammo's team of helpers consisted of all his Comeleg friends and their families, most of his family and a few of the Smiguts.[52] All in

---

all, it was Sammo's friends and family that came to his aid, for the collection of dung had never been a very prestigious occupation, especially in the heat of Fewa[53].

Sammo took the job on with a stout heart and a happy grin. His plans were simple. Dawn reconnaissance at Ealdo the Oak, then head off into teams of four, all equipped with a bag (these bags were pieces of pelt that had been stretched out to about the size of a sheet (a Smidge sized sheet obviously not a human sized sheet). Each of the four Smidge would take a corner, bung the dung in the middle and fly back to Smarahaim with their supplies.

Sammo estimated they would probably make about ten journeys each before Nonahora which calculated into nigh on a score of Smidge and a lot of dung! After luncheon it was twig collecting to make arrows which would take them up to Midafora.[54] Then it would be time to check the bows to ensure the sure strings were strong and pingy.

Everyone who had volunteered (including the Smiguts) turned out at dawn. The dung was collected and given to the Magi to make their potions and the rest of the day fell into place with the utmost

---

53 Summer.
54 Teatime, in the afternoon.

regimen. All in all the day went very well and Silures actually commended Sammo at that Twisk's Smeeting.

At the Smeeting, Silures told the Smidgeon to prepare their bows for battle. The usual day's chores were to be forfeited for collection of dung bombs and armour. Any Smigut over the age of thirty Fews would be expected to join in the campaign. All the remaining Smidgets, Smiguts, Grumpties and Croakles would take refuge in the Grand Hall at Smarahaim awaiting the return of the triumphant Smidgeon.

Chapter 6

Let Battle Commence

At seven breaths before the cock's crow Sammo woke. His dream had returned again that night. Only this time he had fired dung at the Færie Queen, who in turn had thrown a pile of dung back, covering him from head to toe and eventually transforming him into stone. Sammo felt very distressed but could only put the dream down to his Nihealfin[55] of Gatcas Toasties.

The Sun rose up quickly. Sammo packed up Selina, Sashsi and Samus, despite Selina arguing that just because she was with "lumps" she could still throw dung as well as the next Smidge but Sammo would hear none of it. He flew them all down to the Grand Hall at Smarahaim, before joining the rest of the Smidgeon who had begun to assemble on the great platform.

Silures was having forty fits because some of the Smiguts had dyed their hair bright red with the root of the beet as an act of war. However, it was against Smidgeon lore for the colouring of hair, skin or indeed any part of the Smidge body during the hours of the Sun.

---

55   Midnight Feast.

It was common knowledge that it brought too much attention on the Smidgeon by "thems'lot". Silures' eldest son, Silus stepped in.

"S'farva, twill not matter today, there are so many of us. Asides they can tone it down with some dung." Silus said wryly.

The crowd laughed when the Smiguts huffed and crossed their arms with embarrassment as the clan rubbed dung in their hair toning down the red colouring.

Armour, helmets and ammunition were handed out. The Capari[56] drew out from the darkness and depths of Smarahaim, the Bugs of War[57] who protected the Smidgeon. Long gnarly striped creatures with elongated diaphanous wings and vice-like "snappers" were the Werrebucks. Like a strange and dark dragonfly, their flame-red eyes burned in their sockets while their sharp pointed teethfilled mouths gnashed and gnawed as the Capari bridled and saddled them. They hovered menacingly above the growing numbers of Smidgeon. All now waiting for the charge to be called.

Silures stood for a moment as if expecting someone. The Smidgeon looked on and then at each other all shrugging their shoulders as to what or who they were waiting for. Finally, Silures breathed a

---

56   The fishermen who sang the songs of the ancients to lull and calm the Werrebucks/the Bugs of War.
57   Werrebucks.

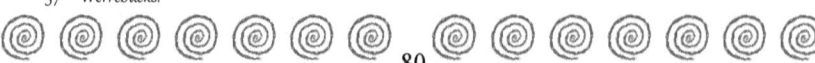

huge sigh as Sinas flew down from the very top branches of Smarahaim.

"What ye waitin' on young Silures?" chuckled Sinas.

"Your Grace we hoped for a blessing before battle commenced." Silures grovelled.

Sinas nodded, ranted a few words under his breath that no-one could hear nor dared to know, for Magi business was not to be tampered with. Then he crossed his staff in the sky, drew a ring about it, crossed it with an "x" and then dotted it. He nodded sharply with an upturned nose at Silures as if to say "that should do you!" and then yelled at the top of his voice "Harkety!" He yelled so hard that his voice broke on the second "Harkety".

"Harkety, Harkety!" he said coughing afterwards. "Tis a brave Smidge that goes a skirmishing, a braver Smidge that lays down a fighting tool, yet tis only a fool that let's "thems'lot" make claim to Smidgeon territory. Fly free, fly high and watch the backs of their pinkins! Let loose the Werrebucks!" and with this he waved his fist. The Smidgeon cheered and flew off to dung bomb "thems'lot".

The Werrebucks lead the charge flying high above the Smidgeon. The Smidgeon en mass, were indeed a sight to behold. Like an eerie

blanket of mist floating across the land. As they reached the gateway, the dry rain could be seen blowing across the small shadows of the morning. Sammo pulled down his goggles and pulled on his scarf. His fellow Comeleggies and close family members had taken his lead and also had scarves to cover their mouths. The Capari blew on the Buculus,[58] as the bugle sounded so the charge began.

Sammo lead his family and friends into the battle. They sped onto the Greylands and through the dry rain. Deafened by the thunder they flew on until they encountered one of "thems'lot", the one that was making the dry rain. They flew about his head shooting their arrows at his neck and ears. He flayed about sending Smidgeon flying.

The Smidgeon fought on forcing him to run off. He waved his arms above his head blindly until he ran into brick wall and collapsed. A few more of "themslot" came running to see what the commotion was. The Smidgeon seized their moment and set upon them. The Capari circling high above began dive bombing, getting close enough for the Werrebucks to sink their teeth into lumps of skin and hair before stinging them with their poisonous pointed tails.

---

58   The Horn of War.

The Smidgeon bombarded them with the dung pellets and before long they had "thems'lot" on the run.

The Smidgeon paused to congratulate themselves but it was a short lived celebration. A booming "manspreking" voice shouted at the four deserters.

"Get back to work!" came the cry from the red-faced portly gentleman who had just stepped out of a very posh car.

Sammo recognised Sir Rusper Chauncey-Bruff straight away and shouted out his command "it's the Baas[59], bomb the Baas!" and the Smidgeon followed Sammo's lead in surrounding Chauncey-Bruff.

They bombed, bit, tore and kicked while Chauncey-Bruff shouted and slapped the air all about him. One workman came to his aid, dragging him kicking and screaming into the builder's hut but still some of the Smidgeon, including Sammo and one of the Capari on the back of a Werrebuck had managed to hold fast.

They continued their fight smearing dung bombs into Chauncey-Bruff's bites. Chauncey-Bruff ran around the room screaming and flailing about, sending Smidgeon flying into the air. He made a quick dash through the open door, back into his car and slammed

---

59   Baas means leader, head of the Clan.

the car door shut behind him. Sammo and a couple of Smiguts sped after him, reaching the car just as it reversed out from the building site.

Sammo managed to grab onto one of the windscreen wipers while the Smiguts gripped with all their might onto the Spirit of Ecstasy figurehead but nearly fainted with fright.

"Ye Gods!" shouted Shenton, his red hair still on show despite copious layers of dung having been slapped onto it.

"Aaarragh!" replied Shontle in agreement.

"They've turned our Lady Queen into a bothering statue!"

They both sat onto their behinds and edged away from the spooky silver statuette. Slowly they moved their way up the bonnet to catch Sammo's attention. Sammo had wedged himself between the bottom of the windscreen and the wiper but was unaware that his scarf had caught on one of the rubber spikes when it began to rain. As Chauncey-Bruff's driver turned on the wipers, poor Sammo had to hold onto the rubber wiper to stop himself from being "stranglulated" as the wiper dragged him up, down and across the window.

Shenton and Shontle watched on in horror as Sammo turned into a fur-ball with each whoosh of the wiper. Finally, Sammo managed to loosen his scarf and prize himself free. He rolled down the slippery window landing face down and spread-eagled in front of a very disturbed Shenton and Shontle, who appeared to be talking gibberish.

A perplexed Sammo desperately tried to understand them, he followed Shenton's shaky finger that was now pointing to the figure of the Silver Lady at the end of the bonnet. Sammo gasped, realising what the Smiguts were trying to tell him. Gingerly, Sammo made his way to the end of the car on all fours, so that he could see with his own eyes. It appeared that Sir Rusper Chauncey-Bruff had indeed murdered the Queen of the Færies. In some sick gesture of "Baasdom"[60], he had set her in silver and now paraded her on the front of his "chareeto[61]" for all to see!

Sammo was incensed. The two Smiguts watched as a red faced Sammo made his way back to the windscreen and ranted, shaking his fists, kicking the window and generally acting very "iree"[62]. This was unusual behaviour for a Smidge, especially for Sammonical Smidge who had the most impeccable manners this side of Smilad.

Suddenly the "chareeto" came to an abrupt halt. Luckily the Smiguts, who had been sitting by the windscreen, captivated by Sammo's outburst, were holding onto the bonnet of the car. Poor Sammo, however, hurtled through the air, passing by the Smiguts like a torpedo.

---

60   Big boss-like behaviour.
61   Car/chariot.
62   Angry and disrespectful.

Fortuitously, Sammo managed to right himself by furiously beating his wings so that he now flew towards the car, changing course so that he narrowly missed being squished into the car park wall. Infuriated, Sammo was relentless, he charged again upon a rather miffed and blotchy Sir Rusper as he sheepishly emerged from his automobile haven. Sammo jumped up and down, tugging at the tufts of red hair on Sir Rusper's balding head.

When the Smiguts joined in, Sir Rusper bolted for cover into "Le Pont du Cassé", the expensive restaurant where Sir Rusper ate regularly. Giving a final swish, Sir Rusper yelled at the top of his voice as he reached the entrance.

"My usual table Stevenson!"

The Head Waiter sprange to life and whisked the jittery gentleman to his "usual table".

"Just bring me my usual everything." Sir Rusper waved him away curtly.

Almost instantly, a bottle of vintage wine and a platter of canapés was placed in front of Sir Rusper but he would have no rest to eat it for Sammo and the Smiguts were flying about his head, shouting

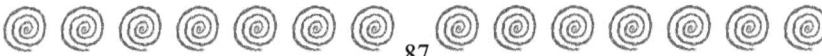

into his ears, kicking, biting, shooting their tiny arrows and rubbing even more dung into the bites and nicks in his face, neck and hands.

Sammo continued to vent his anger. As is often the case with matters of rage, Sammo eventually sailed too close to the wind and he landed "plonk" on the end of Sir Rusper's nose. Sir Rusper's reaction was a natural one, he slapped his hand hard across his chubby red nose, sending Sammo flying.

A winded Sammo landed flat on his back, staring up at a puzzled Sir Rusper who skeptically looked down at Sammo. Sir Rusper tilted his head to one side complete with a baffled expression upon his face as he tried to comprehend what he was seeing.

Looking back at him were a pair of blue enlarged saucer eyes blinking behind a leather mask. Sir Rusper shook his head and rubbed his eyes as Sammo lay motionless with all the puff taken out of him. Stunned, unable to move, Sammo was barely a foot away from Sir Rusper's big ruddy nose and cheeks.

Before Sammo had time to get his breath back and fly off, Sir Rusper placed one of his podgy fingers on Sammo's belly, pinning poor Sammo to the crisp white tablecloth, making it impossible for him to reach into his Pou-da-dew (pouch)[63]. Poor Sammo could not reach for his pouch because Sir Rusper's podgy finger was holding down both his arms and tummy. As Sir Rusper peered at Sammo, the Smiguts circled wildly above looking down, panicking as to what to do. In their confusion, they bumped into each other and in a stroke of catastrophic genius, the two Smiguts mistakenly flew into Sir Rusper's gawping mouth and hit his uvula at the back of his throat, which made him gag and choke.

His coughing then projectiled the pair of Smiguts out and through the air at record speed for any known Smidge. Coughing wildly, Sir Rusper immediately released his hold on Sammo who did not hesitate and instantly took flight. Sammo grabbed a large handful of the doolally dew and blew the dust into Sir Rusper's eyes.

All of a sudden Sir Rusper stopped coughing and looked blankly into space with an odd grin upon his face. Sammo breathed a sigh of relief, grabbed the two Smiguts by their collars and fled the restaurant before they were spotted or before the Smiguts could cause any more chaos.

---

63   A pouch is attached to every Smidgeon belt from the day they take their first breath. In the pouch is the "doolally dew", a fine silvery dust and the Smidgeon's greatest weapon against "thems'lot". One puff of doolally dew in the face of one of thems'lot can induce sneezing fits, followed by feeling of lightheadedness, a "tipsy" sensation, as if you had supped one too many glasses of your Grandma's sherry that she keeps for trifles and special occasions but you're quite happy, slightly queezy and you think everything is marvellous, can't possibly remember your name or where you live but your Mother is due to collect you and you could do with a nice nap by the side of a babbling brook.

They had a long way to fly to return to Smilad. The Smiguts had never been so far away from haim. Even their field trip to the Marshes had not taken them so wide of the borders and without snacks or Sranjey they moaned all the way back.

Sir Rusper on the other hand had behaved in a very odd manner during his stay at the restaurant. In fact, he appeared most unusually polite and charming to everyone until he awoke the next day. The staff at Le Pont du Cassé could not believe the sudden change in Sir Rusper. He even said "thank you" to some of the staff and complimented the chef on all six courses. His chauffeur, "Barrington", had to pile him into the back seat of the car. Barrington presumed Sir Rusper had drunk far too much, as he lay on his back, feet in the air, gurgling and blowing bubbles. Poor Barrington even had to tuck him into bed that night, for Sir Rusper seemed unable to do anything for himself.

It was almost dusky when Sammo and the Smiguts finally returned to Smidgham. Selina, the Smidgets, family and friends were waiting in the village square. Each little face expressed a look of relief when three outlines appeared out of the darkness. The crowd cheered. None of them had washed the dung off as they had been pacing waiting for Sammo's return. The whole village of Smidgham bathed at the Eallpol but not by sunlight, instead they washed under a pale and waxy moon.

Fireflies came and lit their way as they sang of their victorious day. It appeared that the dry storms had been halted, the thunder silenced and "thems'lot" packed off with a flea in their ear.

Sammo kissed Selina and the Smidgets. Breathing a happy sigh, it was all going to be alright.

Chapter 7

And now for the good news...

Sammo had slept a dreamless night. For the first morning in a long time, he woke and smiled outwardly. He and the family sung the Sonsonet, moving and stretching in their Sun Dance but the Sun was not shining today.

They ate Dawnmeall quickly and silently. Poor Sammo could still smell the dung on his hands. It made his meal quite unappetising which was unusual for him, as like all Smidgeon, he loved his food.

"Buzy-nests as usuals." Sammo chirped, kissing the Smidgets and Selina before darting off to work. He collected quickly and efficiently throughout the day until Nonahora when he was due to return to the Greylands. Part of him was hopeful that the Greylands had just disappeared. He strapped down his goggles and fastened his scarf but he could already hear the dull noise of the thunder. His little heart sank and he whispered to himself. "Twas it all in vain?"

Sammo's body ached from the previous day's onslaught. On his travels, he had learned of those Smidgeon who had been less

fortunate in avoiding the swipes of "themslot" and were now "re-co-operating" at haim. There were a few who needed more constant attention and they were being tended to by the Magi at the infirmary at Smarahaim. Sammo really felt like the dung bombing may have been a waste of time.

The future for Smidgeon looked very bleak. Then, suddenly he had a vision. He saw the whole of Smidgeonhood (including those from the four corners of the world) uniting and relocating to a small pond in Frome or even "weirsa" to one of those concrete "zoo-ey-unlogics-call-centres"!

When Sammo reached the Greylands, the thunder was booming and the dry rain teaming. He did not wait to hang about to measure the length of the shadows, he could tell there was no letting up.

At that Twisk's Smeeting Sammo flew lethargically. Shayle Smidge was the Spechan for that Twisk. He rolled off the casualties of the previous day's battle. There were only a few but still too many to have not made the slightest dent in "them'slots" production. It seemed the whole of the Smidgeon flew as torpidly as Sammo. The general feeling was that they had been utterly trounced. Even their motto could not revive them and refreshments after the Smeeting were a very sombre affair.

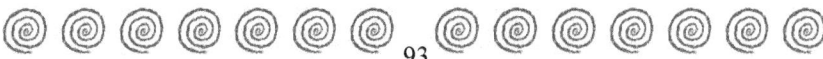

Sammo flew haim, quiet and pensive. He sloped into the Smidget's room without waking them, kissed them both and settled down to Duskmeall. Although he ate heaps, still he could not fill up his heart with the food he loved. Selina sensing his despondency sat silently with him, holding his hand until they retired to bed.

Silures was fast asleep in his bed dreaming of a big portion of Eeleye pie when a knock came at the door. He and his wife, Sibel, sat bolt upright in their bed looking around for intruders. The knock came again, louder, more definite this time.

"By the Færie Queen..." mumbled Silures "it's nearly Nihealf." he whispered loudly into a sleepy Sibel's ear, who looked back at him dumbfounded.

Before Silures had time to reach the door, the knock came again. The handle turned and the door began to creak open. Silures grabbed for a stick and raised up his hand ready to strike. Suddenly he was faced by an eerie looking Sinas, screwing up his nose and squinting passed his rod, which held a swinging lantern.

Sinas looked at a statuesque Silures who was still holding his stick ready for action. "What ye be holding up that for?" Sinas asked Silures who returned an equally quizzical gaze.

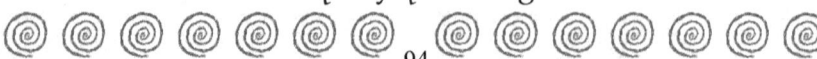

'My... my...my... Lord?" Silures enquired.

"The stick?!" Sinas motioned with his free hand. Silures looked to his lifted hand. Rapidly he lowered the stick and regained his composure although he was still puzzled as to why Sinas would come a knocking at such a late hour.

Before Silures could ask any questions Sinas grabbed Silures by the collar of his nightshirt and proceeded to drag him out of the door.

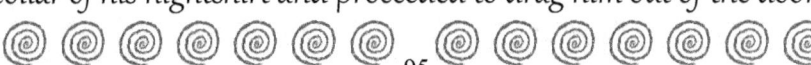

Sibel whispered loudly "Where are ye taking him Lord Sinas?" and Sinas began whispering back before breaking into full voice.

"High Smeeting, of the utmost urgency." Sinas grinned and Sibel grinned a dozey smile back. "Sorry to have troubled ye Sibel, ye can have him back later." and with that Sinas backed out of the door dragging poor Silures with him.

The usual four had been summoned. Sinas dragged a whinging Silures into the Smarahaim Lorechamber where Sharkey, Stoutnose and Shayle were already present. Silures finally stopped complaining about his embarrassment when he saw the others were also in their nightshirts.

Before any of them had a chance to ask questions Sinas launched into a fervid address.

"Tis urgency that brings ye here to me!" he nodded to each of them. "Urgency. We can no longer hold "thems'lot" at bay. My letter should have reached the Isle by now but we can wait no longer for its reply. Tomorrow we must send for help."

The four elders looked at Sinas in bewilderment.

"Glad to see ye are all keeping up!" Sinas chuckled sardonically. "Now Silures my boy, first things first. We need to keep up the dung

bombing. Ye must form teams so the Greylands are constantly attacked. Shayle, I'm putting you in charge of "remediations". We had injuries enough this time but on a constant attack we'll need to be working Sunupsidown[64]. Stoutnose, maintenance of Smilad 1 entrust to you. Keep the Smeetings pithy, let ems know only what they needs to know. Sharkelfrond, dung supplies will be down shortly, I leave you to arrange the collections..." but before Sinas could finish, Sharkey kicked off.

"Dung collections!" Sharkey fumed "Why me?! Let that Sammo Smidge sort it again. He did a sterling job..." but before Sharkey could continue Sinas screwed up his face and yelled back at him.

"I'll hear no more! Be thankful you've haimtasks, for I could send you over to the Scottish Wastes where its frizzin Sunupsidown and your wings drop off from the cold!" Sinas calmed himself and spoke gently to Sharkey "Now, dung collecting is as important as any task. Besides, I canne ask poor Sammo for that is our next task."

Sharkey was still miffed, but listened along with his fellow Magi in anticipation as Sinas revealed Sammo's fate. As the owls called Nihealf, Sinas told them of his plans for Sammo and on the last hoot of the owls, the elders returned to their beds.

---

64   Sun up to Sun down (all day and all night).

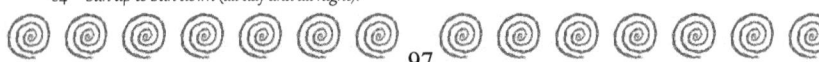

Sammo's dream had returned. The Færie Queen was very large and menacing as she knocked on Sammo's head. Knocking a second time, she called his name in a voice he knew well. Again she knocked, then Sammo realised it was Selina's voice that called him and it was in fact her tapping his head.

"Sammo! Sammo!" she whispered loudly in his ear "There's somebody at the door!" Sammo leapt from their bed and flew down to the main room. Before he had placed the tip of his twinkle toes upon the wooden floor, Sinas was already inside, perched upon a chair, sitting in wait for him.

"Hello again my boy." said Sinas grinning.

"Hello my Lord." Sammo replied rubbing his eyes to wipe the sleep from them (and to see if he was still dreaming).

"I told ye I would see ye again Sammonical." chuckled Sinas as Sammo stared back at him blankly.

"Aye ye did Lord, but I thought ye may have come socialising at a more Sunippy[65] time?"

Sinas laughed and continued "Aye I'm sorry for the intrusion" and he waved to Selina who waved back from around the beddrum door.

---

65 Daytime.

"Sammo I need your help." Sinas said gravely. "I need for you to visit our cousins in the South."

Sammo nodded "No problemo."

Sinas smiled at Sammo's unquestionable willingness. "The Smidgeon depend upon you Sammo, this is your destiny." Sammo nodded again never faltering. "You must visit my brother Sming the Merciful and he will help you to help save Smilad. I can tell you no more except you must take the Widgeon Express to Plymouth and there pick up a connecting Seagull Stopping Service to Tintagel. Someone there will direct you to Sming at Smintagel."

"Oh I see!" sighed Sammo nodding in agreement. Sinas could sense Sammo's fears but he knew that Sammo would say nothing. "What time do I leave?"

"After Dawnmeall laddie. I'll come and take you to the Bridan. I'll have papers of identity for you and notes for my brother." Sinas looked kindly at Sammo. "Till the morrow laddie, till the morrow.".

Like a flash Sinas was out of the door and gone. Selina came flying down to Sammo who stood looking gobsmacked.

"I heard it all Sammo!" she said grabbing him. "Oh my poor Sammo!"

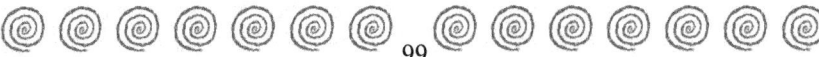

Sammo sighed. "Have no fear my Sluf, all t'will be well, all t'will be well." he muttered leading her by the hand back to bed. As his head hit the downy pillow he slept and dreamt of wings upon the wind.

Chapter 8

All aboard the Skylark!

As promised, Sinas arrived just in time for Dawnmeall. The Smidgets asked him question after question as they sat upon each of his knees.

"We dunna know any cousins down South, Uncle Sinas" Samus chimed as Sinas had been giving the Smidgets a short briefing on their DaDa's important task.

"Ah my cherubs. We have cousins all over the world but our lands diminish with the rise of "thems'lot"." said Sinas raising his eyebrows.

"Does they looks like us?" asked Sashsi.

"All Smidgeon have the same form merely distinctions of locality differ. For example, the Irish Smidgeon have exceptional green hair and rosy pink skin, just like the Piskies. Whereas the Cornish Smidgeon are equally as verdant but their skin is tawny. We are all one big family, separated by land, sea and sky alone."

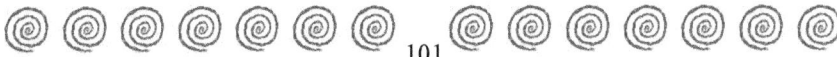

Satisfied by Sinas' explanation the Smidgets prepared themselves for their classes. Selina busied herself making the biggest packed lunch Sammo or Sinas had ever seen.

"I'm not sure the Widgeon Express will be able to take off with such a weighing down, Sluf!" exclaimed Sammo to a despondent Selina.

She wiped her eyes on the knapsack that she tied to the end Sammo's bow, making it bend even more from the weight of its contents. "Come come Sluf." Sammo cuddled her. "I'll be a alrights, I'm always a alrights, I'm your Sammo!" he beamed at her.

"If anything happens to you I'll kill you myself Sammonical Smidge!" she tried to smile but buried her head in his chest to hide her tears.

"Sammo." whispered Sinas. "The day moves on and we can tarry here no longer. The Widgeon Express will not wait." So Sammo grabbed up the Smidgets who were crying, kissing and holding onto him for dear life.

"Be back soon!" waved Sammo with a lump in his throat, for it was the first time he had ventured outside Smilad. He and Sinas marched from Sammo's haim down to the Bridan and good job, for as they arrived at the Bridan, the Widgeon Express flapped down onto the stop.

Sinas handed the bird a bag of small worms he conjured from out of nowhere and whispered something in the bird's ear. Sinas then turned to Sammo.

"Skylark." Sinas said introducing Sammo to the Widgeon Express "Sammonical Smidge" Sinas said introducing the Widgeon to Sammo. Both parties nodded and Sammo grinned hesitantly.

"Off ye go then laddie." Sinas said pointing to the Widgeon who had lifted up his right wing. Underneath, there was a little leather chair. Sammo sat himself down and Sinas strapped him in.

"Ooh before I forget! Papers! By the Færie Queen my marbles are not all in the bag these days!" Sinas handed Sammo a leather wallet. "Have a care Sammo, these hold our fate!" he said winking. "Should anyone ask for your identity, remember this phrase "Ye cam ee hither from the world of merry thither, I'll wander till I whither, whither wonder her I see." Now repeat it after me!" Sinas instructed.

"Ye cam ee hither, from the world of merry thither, I'll wander till I whither, whither wander her I see." beamed Sammo proud he could remember it all.

"No! Tis "wonder" not "wander" on the second! It makes all the difference! Try it again!" Sinas chided.

"Ye cam ee hither, from the world of merry thither, I'll wander till I whither, whither wonder her I see." Sammo said hopefully.

"Perfectamundo Sammonical! By ye Gods I don't know how you were not selected for the Magi! I can see where Sashsi gets it from." Then Sinas whispered again to the Widgeon.

"Now Skylark! This is a delicate package you carry, have a care. Godspeed and may the Færie Queen sprinkle your wings with light." Before Sammo could ask any more questions, Skylark bent his knees and shot off and up into the sky, the wind whistling through his ears.

"My!" thought Sammo. How long it had been since he had taken the Bridan to school like his Smidgets now did. He had forgotten what it felt like to be carried upon the wind without using his own wings.

Widgeon's are known for their speed for they couriered between the Emerald Isle and Smilad daily. The legendary Silver Pullet had flown non-stop to break all records for the fastest round-trip. A title the Silver Pullet had held onto for over a hundred years and which was still to be beaten.

Skylark was fleet. He zoomed into the clouds and hit a Southerly flowing stream of wind, heightening their speed further. Sammo had been smiling but now found it hard to close his mouth because the current of air beat so fiercely against his face. It was ice cold up so high, Sammo pulled his wings about himself. It shielded the chill of the wind and stopped him from freezing to death, although his teeth chattered and his fingers felt burnt as the icy clouds gathered around them.

Everywhere was white, pure white. Sammo was unsure how long they had been travelling or how far they had to go, for he could not make out any landscape. He rested his head upon Skylark's tummy, it was warm and fluffy. Although Sammo thought he was too cold to even sleep, he drifted off within moments.

Suddenly he was running again, there was something colossal towering over him and as he looked up a giant shadow was looming down, about to crush him. Sammo woke with a start, his arms flaying about as he tried to shelter from another disturbing dream. He recovered quickly and just in time, before he lost his knapsack.

Fully awake now, Sammo breathed a sigh of relief.

Skylark tipped, turning left to alight from the Southern stream. They were heading into the West. Suddenly they were out of the clouds and flying into a beautiful sunny day. Below them the ground was a verdant luscious green. A warm stream of air washed over Sammo as they picked up the Zephyr, the wind route that would take them all the way to Plymouth. Putting his dream far behind him, Sammo felt excited and alert.

Sammo could tell from the sun that they had been travelling for the best part of the morning and that he must have slept most of the way after all. It was not very long before Skylark lowered and Sammo could hear lots of different noises.

There were boats, cars and hundreds of "them's lot". Sammo started to panic a little. He had not expected to be taken to their Kingdom. Fortunately, Skylark turned off again and soon they were flying over a green field that held a single tree with a stream flowing gently by its side. Skylark set down by the stream and Sammo disembarked.

Skylark was not remotely out of breath as he turned to Sammo and said "Record time! Broken me own personal best 1 'ave."

Sammo smiled politely.

"I'm after the Silver Pullet's crown this year, been in training all winter, reckon I'm good for it though." said Skylark whilst Sammo nodded continually like a fool. "You want the Tintagel Stopping

Service now. That's Eric. He's usually late. Always catches a bite on the way y'see." Sammo nodded again "Well then mate, I'll be off, may see you on the way back but then it might be Lightning. Humpf...Lightning indeed, it'll take you twice as long wiv 'im!" and with that Skylark shot off and up into the sky.

Sammo looked around him. All was silent, except for the babbling of the stream. It felt a little like Smilad but without the magik. There were no Smidgeon here. There had been, but they had long since departed.

He missed Selina and the Smidgets. Opening up his packed lunch he laughed heartily. There was a slice of Eeleye Pie, a chunk of Grubs-Up, three sliced pieces of bread with Gatcas and four slices of bread covered in Moochi. All to be washed down with a jar of Ealu.

"Oh Selina how I love thee." thought Sammo to himself.

Skylark was right. The time he had made up getting Sammo to the Plymouth stop (mid-morning) had soon been lost. The Tintagel Stopping Service (or Eric as he preferred to be called) did not turn up until Nonahora[66]. Sammo was surprised to find that Eric was not a Widgeon but a big old Seagull, complete with a long yellow

---

66   High Noon.

beak and matching eyes. He was a bit short-sighted so he almost left without Sammo.

"Hey-up! Hallooooh!" Sammo shouted up to him.

Eric looked around.

"Hallooooh! Down here!" Sammo boomed.

Eric finally looked down to see Sammo frantically waving at him.

"Ah there ye be! My my ... I keep forgetting how teensy you's lot are!" Eric chuckled. Despite Eric being a big scarey bird, he had a nice manner about him.

"Ye cam ee hither, from the world of merry thither, I'll wander till I whither, whither wonder her I see." Sammo said to Eric who now had his beak at Sammo's feet.

"Eh? What's that laddie?" Eric asked.

"Password?!" Sammo offered.

"Oh. You can save that for yourslot. Tickets please!" said Eric lifting up his long grey and white wing and motioning for Sammo to get into one of the little leather chairs. Sammo checked through all the papers that Sinas had given him but he could not find a ticket.

"I...I...don't seem to have...have a ticket?" Sammo said beginning to worry.

"Never mind then!" said Eric, jostling Sammo toward the seats with his beak. Eric waited while Sammo strapped himself in and then launched up into the blue of the sky.

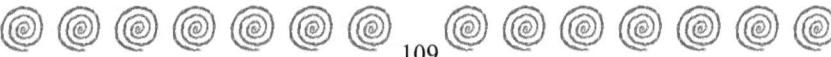

Skylark, was indeed again right, it was a much slower flight than the Widgeon Express but then again the Widgeon was an "express" and Eric was the Tintagel stopping service. Although there seemed to be no other passengers to pick up, Eric still stopped at every stop.

First was Looe where no-one got on, then Liskeard where another Smidge got off (apparently, he had been sitting under the other wing all the time). At Bodmin Moor, Eric became anxious. There was one pick up, a Smigut with long spikey bright green hair (green hair is typical of the Cornish clan) who dashed out from the tree stop as Eric landed.

"Quick quick!" Eric squawked. "That beast is around again, poor Ernie got his wings clipped last night!" Eric's urgent tone seem to do the job as the Smigut jumped into the seat next to Sammo and buckled himself in rapidly. Eric then sped off towards Wadebridge.

"How do?" said the Smigut once they were out of the danger zone.

"Hallo." replied Sammo.

"Not from around these parts are ye?" asked the Smigut.

"Nay, I is from Smilad." Sammo said.

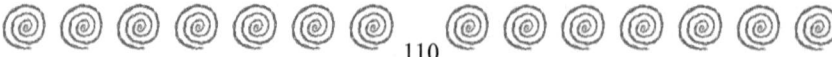

"Smilad!" yelped the Smigut. "My S'farva's Grumpties were from Smidgington! We're probabs relat-tized! I'm Souzel." Sammo and Souzel then had a lovely chat about the market at Smidgeham and Smaharaim.

Eric swooped into Wadebridge and picked up two old Grumpties. He insisted that they sit under his other wing so he was properly balanced, otherwise, he explained they could be going around in circles until the end of time. As Eric dipped into Camelford and the Grumpties disembarked. Sammo began to tell Souzel about the Greylands.

"Now "thems'lot" have a lots to answers for, I can tell 'eee!" said Souzel.

"Well that's whys I'm here!" Sammo said proudly. "I'm here to meet with Sming the Merciful!"

"That's my Great, Great, Great, Great, Great .... Great.... Great Uncle!" exclaimed Souzel " but I just call him Uncle. That's 'mazen?! I can takes ye right to 'im, cos this stop is a bit away from the village likes."

As Eric swooped down onto Tintagel, the last rays of sun were waning, the castle ruins a silhouette against a majestic backdrop of the crashing ocean.

"All off!" shouted Eric. Sammo and Souzel only just had time enough to unbuckle themselves and slide out before Eric swished off and out to sea for his supper.

Chapter 9

Sming the Merciful

"Come on Sammo!" Souzel beckoned.

Sammo followed Souzel down a sandy path away from the coastline. As the land dipped, they came to a Cornish stone wall. Souzel took a key from his pocket and put it into the wall. A stone door opened and Souzel ushered Sammo through into a dark musky passageway.

Suddenly Sammo became anxious, what if Souzel was a "trickster". He had not given Souzel the password and Souzel had not asked for it. Sammo felt like running but Souzel was too quick and the stone door was closed and locked behind them leaving them both in total darkness.

"Ooops!" Souzel gasped. It was pitch black and Sammo could not see a thing. All he heard was shuffling and scraping around him. Sammo prayed to the Færie Queen for help. Then with a great deal more scratching and scuffling round, Souzel finally appeared from another passage with a lantern in his hand.

"Should have lit this first! I always forgets!" he guffawed. "This way Sammo." Souzel said chirpily, skipping down the passage. Sammo had no choice but to follow, for behind him was nothing but a dark void. The passage wound down and around and soon they were so far down Sammo thought they may come out on the other side of the world.

It was not too long before there was a dim orange light ahead of them. As they reached the end of the passage the view took Sammo's breath away. In front of him was the Sun. A great round orb, dipping itself into a red stained ocean, casting its orange rays across the world.

The ruins were much nearer now. Souzel drew Sammo's attention to the hillside and a small plateau, where no human foot would ever step. Smintagel village sat on the edge of the cliff face. Sammo could see lights being turned on in the little haims. Suddenly all his fears of Souzel and abduction swiftly left him and he felt churlish for being so mistrustful.

Souzel took off and flew to the ledge, for there was no other way of getting there. He motioned to Sammo, who eventually followed

along behind, breathing in the salty sea air. When they reached the centre of the plateau, Sammo saw the town square where the Smidgeon of Smintagel would carry out their festivals.

"My Uncle will be in his study. Shall I take ye to him now or would ye like to eat?" asked Souzel.

"Ooh I should really meets with Sming the Merciful now, for I have urgent errands!" Sammo pressed.

"Righto Sammo! Follow us then petsie." Souzel sped off under a great arch which had been cut into the side of the cliff. Lights were being lit as Souzel weaved Sammo in and out of the intricate labyrinth of streets and avenues. Finally, Souzel stopped at a large wooden door. He rapped on the metal knocker that was moulded into the shape of a skull. Sammo gulped and his anxieties returned as the door opened into darkness.

Once inside the haim, Sammo saw that he was in the middle of a large study. The walls were lined from top to bottom with books, parchments, bottles, jars and odd looking instruments.

"Uncle Smingel" shouted Souzel.

It seemed just by their entering the room they had set the dust to fly. It clung to Sammo's nose and he began to sneeze.

"Uncle Smingel!" Souzel shouted harder.

"What in the Færie Queen! Souzel! How many times do I have to tell ye not to shout or ye'll wake the Tommy Knockers!" Sming's voice resonated out from a room at the back of the study.

The owner of the voice appeared behind a pile of book and Sammo then took a double take for Sming looked very much like Sinas, but with longer hair, tied back into a ponytail. Unlike Sinas, Sming did not limp, in fact he was extremely spritely for such a very old Smidge.

"Ooooh and who are you?" Sming said looking down his glasses at Sammo.

"Ye cam ee ...hither from the world of merry ...thither, I'll ...wander till I whither, whither wonder her I see!" Sammo blurted out.

"Yes yes yes, very nice but who are ye?" Sming asked.

"Sammo from Smidgeham." he offered.

"Sammo from Smidgeham. Well ye be a long way from haim. What brings ye to Smintagel?" asked Sming.

"..S..Sin..Sinas sent me." Sammo said hopefully as Sming narrowed his eyes in reservation.

"Sinas sent ye? Is this more codebreakers? Ye Feie Gomshum! What the begibblings are you on about? I can't work this out!" said Sming scratching his head.

"Sinas? Your brother? From Smarahaim?" Sammo said optimistically.

"Sinas?" Sming said as if he had not heard that name in an age "Sinas sends ye?"

"Aye" nodded Sammo. "He gave me these to give to ye." Sammo took the rolls of parchment and letters that Sinas had given to him, offering them to Sming, who still looked on in bewilderment.

Sming finally took the papers and read through them. Occasionally he would glance back at Sammo through narrowed eyes until he had read everything.

'Mmmm. Funny he never mentions ye in any of this!?" Sming said suspiciously.

Sammo gulped as Sming drew closer. It appeared that he was on trial.

"I have had no news of ye? Ye could be an Escheat[67]!?"

"...bur...but...but ...er...I...I...was sent by Sinas..." babbled poor Sammo wringing his sweaty palms together.

"I have no news of ye, no word of ye, nowt so much as a whisper, token or letter..."

"Oh talking of letters..." interrupted Souzel casually handing Sming a bundle of letters. "....today's post."

Sming looked cagily at Sammo as he sifted through the mail until he came across a small blue envelope. He nodded and scratched his head. Then gasped and scratched his head some more. Sming then

67   Trickster.

ran back into the room behind the study and started pulling books off of the shelves. He began to open jars, taking out some of the contents, dropping it all into a mortar and then grinding with a pestle.

Souzel looked at his Uncle with a baffled expression and shrugged his shoulders at fretful Sammo who was equally mystified.

Sming's manner was now one of urgency and he began shouting out orders to them both "get me this...", "fetch me that herb ...", "where's the gravy..." "give me some doolally dew quickly, just a pinch...".

Thankfully, Sming's initial intimations that Sammo was a spy, had been forgotten and he now frantically busied himself grinding, sprinkling and pounding strange coloured liquids and stinking oils that blew smoke and bubbled up.

Eventually, after some time Sming sighed a happy smile. He nodded to himself as he poured a lavender coloured liquid into a small phial. He then turned to Souzel and said "Right off ye go and tell your S'muvva to sets another mound at the table."

Souzel ran off to tell his mother to prepare for a guest.

Sming swung around, his beady eyes fixed intently on Sammo.

"So! Ye be the hope of us all Sammonical Smidge?" Sming roared.

"I...I...I...don't know what ye mean?" said Sammo nervously, his big blue eyes blinking in wonder.

"Tis no matter. My brother Sinas is as wise as the wisest owl that hoots the Nihealf. Mmm... thinking of Nihealfin, ye hungersome young Sammo?" said Sming in a much more amenable tone.

"Aye." said Sammo smiling for the first time at the thought of food.

Sming put the phial in a cupboard and scurried back to Sammo brushing him along and out of the study into the twilight. Sming breathed in deeply "Ooh, tis Twisk, time for the Smeeting, hurry laddie, a hovering we must go."

Sming flew off and down the cliff face, over the rock pools to where the Smidge of Smintagel held their Smeeting.

Sammo was excited. He had never attended a Smeeting at any other Smidgeon settlement, but then, he had never left Smilad before. Also, although he was on an important errand, it felt a bit like being on holiday. There were different faces and he had not a care in the world as he swished in and out singing the opening songs of the Smeeting.

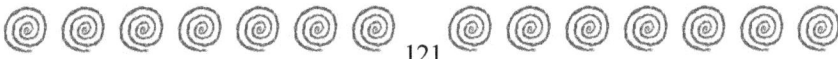

As he hovered and listened to the "Harketies!" he realised how much he was missing Selina and the Smidgets, but before he could grow any gloomier a "Harkety!" was called.

"Harkety!" cried the Spechan again. "Be welcoming to Sammonical Smidge from Smidgeham!" and the throng all looked to Sammo and clapped and nodded their welcome.

"Sammonical is here on urgent buzy-nests. "Them'slot" have been at its agains! Smidginton is under shadow and the land of Smilad is at great threat!"

The mob of Smidgeon gasped at the terrible news and began to chatter. As the Sun slowly sank beneath the Ocean, the low hum of voices wafted out to sea and the Smeeting came to a close.

Chapter 10

Ring a Ring a Færie Queen

Smintagel, like all Smidgeholdings, had a fountainheart[68] at its centre with haims off of its core. Sming flew Sammo to his Great, Great, Great, Great, Great Granddaughter's haim, Souzette. Souzette and her husband, Sinton, had been blessed with a hoard of Smidgets who were all fully grown and flown except Souzel, who fairly drove both this Smidge parents almost "doolally tat!"

The whole of Sming's family ate together, which was wonderful for Sammo as it reminded him of Suneall at Ye Old Smidirin. Only trouble was, it did not leave a lot of standing room let alone sitting room. All in all there was a lot of hullabaloo and the Duskemeall went on well into Nihealf.

They delighted telling Sammo of the stories of the dragon that used to bide deep in the caves under the Castle and of Arthur and Merlin. They scared the wits out of him with the ghost stories of the lost Knights who could not find their way back to Camelot and the wails of the Buckas.

---

68   Village Square.

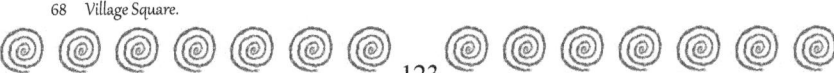

But the most terrifying news that night, came from Sammo's mouth. As he supped from his umpteenth tankard of Snacabitan he jovially informed everyone that he was off to visit the Færie Queen.

First of all, everyone fell about laughing but as Sammo continued, Sming nodded seriously and so the mood of the room darkened.

"Tis not been done since yonder Battle of 1856, up at Swale where the Piskies had to be called in to oust out those rogue guppies, cos of some idiot "thems'lot" tippsying narkinstuff[69] in 'ter Swale estuary..." said Souzette.

"Nay, last time be 1967 of "thems'lot"! The 1967 Invasion of Isle of Sheppey by Gargoyles from Minster Abbey! Dontcha 'members? "Thems'lot" up to undo-handy!" chipped in Sinton. "Blaecwicca[70]! The wiersa magik!" and everyone shuddered.

"Aye." interjected Sming. "Tis always "thems'lot" that dabbles with stuff they's know nuffinks of. Blaecwicca indeed." he tutted and shook his head with the utmost displeasure.

Sammo's eyes were wide as he nervously regarded Sming.

---

69   Chemical waste.
70   Black Magic.

"Now laddie. Ye need no fear." said Sming. "Tis but a simple course and one which we must make for an early start so ye and thee will bid these 'orribles "Goodly Biniht"" he said winking at Souzette.

Sammo followed Sming out of Souzette and Sinton's haim and into the crisp night air. The moon was almost full, round and creamy.

"Oooh just as I hoped." whispered Sming with glee in his eyes as he pointed to the moon. "Tomorrow brings a full new one, the Gods smile on us. Sinas did well to send ye at this time. Come Sammo, ye need to get little rest before the task at hand."

Sming showed Sammo to his only beddrum. Sammo gulped. For a split second he thought he may have to share a hammock with Sming.

Luckily the old Smidge rocked the hammock to and fro and smiled at him. "Restie byes, bysie, bysie laddo." then he flew out of the beddrum window leaving Sammo to look out and up at the creamy moon hanging over the Ocean. He could see the face of Lunami, the Moon Goddess and he prayed to her to bring him haim safely to all his kith and kin.

When his head hit the pillow, the world began to spin. As the ocean waves lapped against the cliff it lulled Sammo into a deep and heady sleep.

Sammo thought he could have barely been asleep for a moment when Sming came to wake him again. It was still dark but the moon was falling into the West.

"Come come." whispered Sming. "The time is now."

Sammo flew out of the hammock and followed Sming who was already flying off up past the original gateway where Souzel had brought him. They flew down past the rock pools and then back up towards the ruins. The air was cold and damp and Sammo was puffed out unsure how much further he could fly when Sming finally stopped on top of a large flat stone.

The moon was shining so brightly that Sammo could see markings upon the stone. Illuminated by the moon's rays seemed to be some kind of strange writing.

Sming brought out a huge manuscript and began to recite in Fiera.[71] Sammo stood watching and waiting, but nothing happened. Sming then bade him to follow him towards a large

---

71 The language of the Færie Queen.

grassy mound. Here he repeated the language and sprinkled some dust and muck onto a gust of wind that seemed to have come out of nowhere. Shivers ran down Sammo's back.

Under Sming's direction they walked anti-clockwise around the mound and Sming chanted as he walked ahead. Sammo was shuddering from the cold and his head was hurting. By the time they were halfway around the mound Sammo was feeling quite bored and believed Sming to be quite "barking" mad. Still they both trudged until they stopped where they had first started.

Nothing.

Sammo grimaced in an attempt to smile politely but Sming was not even remotely perturbed that nothing was happening.

He handed Sammo the phial of lavender coloured liquid. Sammo smelled it. It had an awful stench that it made Sammo want to be sick. Sammo handed it back to Sming who pushed his hand away and bid him drink it.

Sammo was horrified but Sming somehow cohersed the phial to his lips. Sammo gingerly opened his mouth and Sming gave Sammo's elbow a quick tap so that Sammo ended up with a mouthful of the concoction. Sming nodded for Sammo to swallow the liquid.

At this point, Sammo looked like a hamster with his cheeks full of food. Sammo shook his head refusing to drink, so Sming pinched his nose and gave his throat a quick flick leaving Sammo no choice but to gulp down the revolting potion.

There was still half of the liquid left in the phial which Sming drained and drank as if it were honeydew. He then nodded for Sammo to follow him again.

Sming continued around the mound. A gust of wind blew up again, helping them around the mound as if there were invisible hands at their backs. Still absolutely nothing seemed to be happening.

Then Sammo had a damp cold feeling. It started in his twinkle toes and rose up to his head as if he were being filled up with ice cold water. He began to feel quite ill. They were still walking around the mound but now the mound appeared to be shrinking so that it was now flat and level. There were odd sparks flying out of the earth. As they continued their slow trudge, a multitude of rings emerged, winding outwards from the centre. As Sammo looked down he realised he was walking on one of the rings and that it was illuminated with a bright verdant glow.

He tried to get off of the ring but his legs would not let him. The grass had vanished and below his twinkle toes was a path of shimmering silver pebbles that snaked towards the centre which was now spiraling downwards.

Around and around they both traipsed and the path became wider.
What at first had been a small ridge continued to grow into a
partition, rising with every step, until it became a high stone wall
covered in dark green shimmering moss and ivy lit only by the
moonlight.

Sammo felt sure he could not take another step when they rounded
a bend and came face to face with a huge ironclad door.

Sming unruffled by any of their journey so far looked back at Sammo who swayed from side to side, as he looked up, agog, at the great blockade in front of them.

"Howzgwegoonagetsthrewthere..." Sammo slurred.

Sming began to rant his chant again and the great heavy door clicked and Sming effortlessly pushed it open. Sammo hiccupped out loud. All his fears and trepidations were no longer with him. In fact, he was quite looking forward to meeting her Ladyship.

Once through the doorway it became very dark. Not a sound could be heard except the beating of their tiny hearts. Sammo hiccupped

again but Sming's mood had changed somewhat, for he turned to Sammo and put his forefinger to his lips to motion for Sammo's silence. Sming's beady eyes were alert as he scanned the blackness. As they continued onwards the darkness gradually lifted to be replaced with a soft green hue.

"We have entered the Feielands so we must have a care laddie. T'will be a short while before we reach the Færie Wood where we may seek counsel with the Lady." Sming whispered.

Suddenly, two large hounds bound out from nowhere, barking their angry tone. They were Hera and Vega the twin dogs of the Goddess Anisamon who guarded the Feielands. They were the size of small ponies, with long wirey black hair and their ears drawn back from demon red eyes. Gnashing and snarling their foaming jaws, Sming instantly took flight but Sammo weaved around on the ground narrowly avoiding a lethal bite, until he finally remembered he could fly and how to make his wings work again!

Sammo missed death by a hare's breath and caught up with Sming who was forging ahead, looking back at him, shaking his head and mumbling something about "sending a Smigut to do a Smidgeon's work".

Sammo huffed irritably and flew after Sming. And fortunately so for Sammo, as one of the hounds leapt up, teeth gnashing in an attempt to catch Sammo in its jaws. After such a narrow escape, Sammo's lightheadedness disappeared but he still felt jittery, until the barking of the hounds abated, leaving just the eerie silence.

Sammo found the Feielands much more sinister and claustrophobic than he had expected. The dull green surroundings throbbed rhythmically, pulsating through his body. Sming continued speedily forward over a swampland, covered by a low mist that hung above the strange and menacing mere.

Every now and then the sound of something moving around in the water could be heard followed by the snapping of a large set of teeth. Bright green and blue dragonflies zoomed up from out of the mist. Relentlessly, Sming flew them both onward, toward a copse of trees that now loomed in the distance.

Drawing closer to the woodland, Sammo could see it was shaped in a circle. Two of the trees appeared to make a natural gateway. Sming assessed the entrance and stopped just in time as two Spriggans leapt up from out of nowhere, looming high above them. The two Smidge would have flown straight into their thick grey furry chests had Sming not been prepared. Instead Sming grabbed

Sammo and they both weaved around the two hairy beasts avoiding capture by their large clawed mitts.

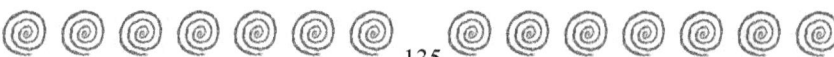

But Spriggans are no match for the spritely Smidgeon and before too long Sming and Sammo left them far behind as they weaved their way deeper into the Færie Wood.

Chapter 11

Don't mention the War!

On they flew. Sammo constantly looked behind in fear that the Spriggans or the dogs may be in pursuit. But they were alone. The deeper they flew into the woods so the darker green it became along with a heady scent that filled the air.

Suddenly spread out before them was a sea of bluebells covering the vista with a colour so bright that Sammo had to cover his eyes. Their fragrance was so sweet and pungent it almost made Sammo want to lay down and sleep but Sming dragged him towards a leafy glade.

The dell was lush green and at its centre were two large monoliths. Between the monoliths sat a flat round stone. Sming and Sammo landed amid the bluebells and surreptitiously peered out. It was very quiet.

Too quiet.

Sming muttered "Tis nothing for it..." and he proceeded very slowly to walk to the monoliths. Sammo's knees trembled with dread. Little by little they edged closer to the stones. Feeling exposed, they walked as fast as they dare without bringing too much attention upon themselves althought Sming sensed there were eyes upon them.

Still nothing.

They reached the centre of the stone plateau and stood, waiting. The markings upon the stone had the mark of the Fiera, elaborate circles focused around the centre circle.

Sming looked at the markings and sighed. "Tis a long time since I camee hither. Time for you to speak the words Sinas bade ye say laddie."

Sammo cleared his throat, not sure if he could remember them.

"Ye cam ee hither from the world of merry thither, I'll wander till I whither, whither wonder her I see." Sammo repeated the phrase confidently, surprising even himself.

Nothing happened. All was deathly quiet. Unnervingly so.

"Right Sammo, tis time to start the walk again." said Sming who then began to walk around to the centre of the carved ring. Before they had got halfway they were stopped in their tracks.

"Who beckons she?" came a distant voice, full of light and wonder.

"The Smidgeon bid guidance from the Ladye." Sming bellowed back.

"Do ye indeed!" the voice now came from above them. There, floating like a feather upon the breeze, was the Queen of the Færies. She was surrounded by her people, all of who now looked sternly down on Sming and Sammo.

The Queen was more beautiful than Sammo could have ever have imagined possible. He had seen lots of "thems'lot" and the Queen stood about the same height as one of the tall humans, just under six feet but no mortal could compare to this Lady. Nor indeed could any of the Smidgeon come close to the splendour of the Færie Queen.

A throne appeared in front of the two rock pillars. The Queen of the Færies took her place upon it. There she sat, her dark ringlets framing a lilywhite face that shimmered and sparkled. Her green eyes were vigilant and all knowing. Soft pink and lilac diaphanous

robes hung loosely about her like petals upon a rose and her crown of dewdrops glistened on top of her head, icy and frosty just as was her manner toward these miniscule envoys.

"So?" she enquired seemingly irritated.

"We bid your Lady the highest accalaidations, triple tribulations, many consternations, that bring us Smidgeon to bide at your side for comfort and servitude..."

"Enough Sming! What is it ye want?" she snapped.

Sming was dumbstruck. He could not believe that she would know his name or even remember him. He had been but a Smigut when he first paid visit to these lands, many many leagues ago, under the study of his Master who begged counsel for the Battle of 1856 at Swale.

"er...er... erm... your Ladyship does me such accoladatary....."

"Get on with it Sming, ye be wasting my time." she barked at him.

"We...ell...we...we....we... have come in hope that ye may save Smilad from the blight of Mankind..."

"Yes, yes, yes!" she closed her eyes "What of them?"

"Well, "thems'lot" are buildings haims and flattening the last of the midland Smidgeon, twill be murder sure enough..."

"And ye expect us to do what exactly?" she said sardonically.

"Tis all the folk at Smidgeham, Smidgington, and Smarahaim..."

"Smarahaim?" she uttered through softer lips and narrowed eyes.

"Aye, the old one!" he offered with hope.

She shook her head and laughed mockingly scoffing at them.

"Ye think that after all this time, we could help ye? Arbitrate upon yeself?" she continued to shake her head in disbelief. "The last time ye were here, we told ye, t'would be the last!" she leapt out of her throne, drew alongside the stone circle, bent down and pushed her face close to the two Smidge, glowering.

"I told ye never to darken the Feielands again or be sure of death. The most I can do for ye is to spare yonder lives, worthless they be, now be gone damn irritant! Get thee away and back to thy worthless haims!" she recoiled and began to return to the Feielands with her people.

The meeting over, Sammo turned to Sming and said "Well?! Tell her this is an emergence!"

Sming shook his head. His body showed how weary he really was. He had given his all but now he was hollow and seemed without hope or expectation.

"Her word is final." Sming said deflated, he turned to leave the Færie Woods.

"Is it indeed!" said Sammo and he took off after the Queen.

"Oi! Oi! Lady Queen! Oi!" he flew up about her face.

"What in Par's name!" she shouted, trying to bat him away with her hand. Her people surrounded her and tried to catch him but remarkably Sammo dodged any efforts of capture.

"Now ye listen to me your highness, my family are being trodden off and scrumpled up and tis down to ye to sort it out..."

Suddenly she rose up, shining from the inside out, so bright just like a star.

"Ye listen to me trystups!" her voice thundered and Sammo thought he was going to die on the spot. "The Smidgeon made their choice the day we set sail for the West, to these Woods where ye bide now. Ye all had the choice, now ye live and die in the beddrums ye made for yeself. Ye turned upon your own, ye be turncoat, no better than the warlock, live and die by the Fiera or live and die alone..." she snarled and turned her back upon him again, as she walked away.

Sammo knew not where his gusto came from but he followed after her.

Sming stood wide-mouthed as Sammo continued to give chase and launched again at the Færie Queen with an acidic diatribe. All Sammo could think was that this creature had called him a "traitor" and he was having none of it.

"Now listen to me ye witch!" shouted Sammo.

The Queen of the Færies turned on her heel. The Færie folk stood fast stunned at his effrontery.

"Aye the Smidgeon had the chance to come and live 'ere'aslike in Feielands, living out our days harmoniouso-so-so, but we wudna

give up on the world like ye's lot did. Ye just left. Ye didney care for the trees. Ye gave no concern for the Bovies and ye made damn sure the Brownies cudney stay to keep the magik. Ye spoilt it all because ye lost ye faith in the world." lambasted Sammo. "The Smidgeon stayed throughout all the war and postulations, in fear and hopeless like, but cos of tyrranicals we stayed and have puttupity for scaremongers otherwise t'would be lost forever. Ye be "ickmush"[72] and if ye can stand by and watch as Smarahaim dwindles and passes forever into the Summerlands then I spit on ye..." and he turned and flew off his head held high.

Sming waited and watched the Queen. Her face gave nothing away. Sming knew she could squash Sammo without even looking at him, but instead she laughed. She laughed loud and Sammo stopped to turn to see what all the fuss was about. Her people were looking at her in wonder.

"Sammo?" she called softly. "Sammonical Smidge?"

Sammo hovered upright with his arms crossed tapping one of his twinkle toes in mid air. The Queen laughed it him again.

"So tis not dead then?" she asked softly.

---

72 Selfish.

"What tisnut dead?" Sammo asked.

"The old Smidge Magik, the Smidgeon Spirit?"

Sammo put his head down for he felt himself blushing. He laughed an embarrassed laugh and when he looked back at her she was smiling. Now she was being kind she was even more beautiful. Sammo felt shy and self-conscious.

"T'will never die all the while Smarahaim breathes." he whispered.

"Ah! The old one. Ye knew if ye mentioned her I'd yield did ye not?"

"T'was a long shot my Lady!" Sammo bowed.

The Queen chuckled again.

"Come Sming, Sammo, let us take Fieradu[73] and discuss what has to be done. Ye know Sammo ye really are the bravest of the Smidgeon I have ever met." She said putting out her hand for them both to land on.

---

73   Fairy Dew – the drink of the Færies – a bit like very sweet tea.

Sammo reddened again. Sming despite feeling distrustful of the Queen, could not help but bang on Sammo's arm, beaming with pride and admiration.

Chapter 12

Bring on the Prancing Brownies

"I dunna what came over me Sming." whispered Sammo.

"Dunne matter laddie, it did the jobbins!" Sming whispered back happy that they may get help after all.

The Queen took them between the two monoliths. Once inside, the forest took on a whole different panorama. There was so much vitality and noise that it made you want to burst with excitement.

Sming sighed and smiled sadly. "I remember t'was beauteous here but nay did I not remember so well..."

She led them far past the gateway, which had now strangely disappeared. On towards a spiralled city that gleamed in the sun. The journey seemed to take just moments for suddenly they were within the City Walls, being escorted into a large hall and into the throne room. Here the Queen bid them sit on the smallest Smidgeon chairs and had refreshments brought to them. Then she

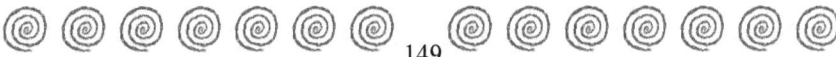

amazed them by shrinking to the size of a large Smidge so that she could have Fieradu with them.

At first, the conversation was full of pleasantries. The Queen seemed extremely taken by Sammo who continued to blush at every question. He had lost his new-found zest and now shuddered at his outburst and apologised profusely.

"Come come now Sammo, t'would not be sitting supping withst me if ye had not! Now to business. Tell me what ails those of Smilad?"

"Well ye worship, tis "thems'lot". Every day the dry rains pour and the noise and the shadows grow so that Smidginton is almost under darkness. We tried the dung bombing and that didney stoppum and now Selina is having twins again and all the Smidgets and Smiguts in Smarahaim..."

"Calm down Sammo!" she reassured him.

"bur....bur...but "thems'lot" are eirrie and getting wiersa..."

"Forget not this, l am as old as the eldest and as wise as the wisest, l was there at their creation when the Demon God spilled his own vile blood into the melting pot giving them the flaws and inconsistencies they have to this day. Ye will never change man but ye may disrupt and trick him. Remember Sammo, the mind of man has been

closed to our kind. They bade us goodbye in the dark ages and will have nout said about us." She patted his arm and turned to summon her courtier. "Bring the whistle." Moments later the courtier returned with a small whistle. She had to grow slightly taller to blow it, in fact she grew to the size of a large Brownie.

She only had to blow it once when the pounding of paws and high howling could be heard in the distance. Instantly, two small brown men, about a foot in size came tearing through the castle grounds on the back of a large brown dog.

"Ye called m' Lady!" said the taller of the two.

"Oh Ossie, I'm glad tis ye." the Queen smiled.

The small brown man bowed low and tipped his brown fur cap.

"And Madcap, how have ye been? Is Mrs Fingle on the mend?"

"Aye." nodded Madcap who was marginally shorter and quite stout with ruddy cheeks that broke into an infectious smile. "She's up and running 'bout 'gains, now the triplets are on the boviedrincan."

"Oooh triplets was it?! How wonderful!" the Queen beamed.

"Smidgeon, may I take this opportunity to introduce ye to Ossie de Brunt and Madcap Fingle. Ossie, Madcap this is Sming the Merciful of Smintagel and Sammonical Smidge of Smidgeham. I have a task for ye, will ye take it?" she looked hopefully at the Brownies.

"Yep!" nodded Ossie.

"Without asking t'what it be?" she offered.

"We'll do it." grunted Madcap. "If they be's 'ere, then tis to go back through yonder and sort out the mess no doubts?"

"Brownies!" exclaimed the Queen. "Ye really are the most delightful. Bide till dusk, then I shall have the potions and instructions then ye must head for the haim of the Smidgeon."

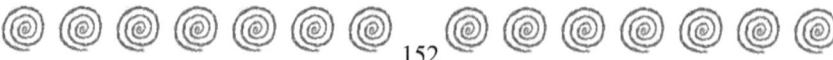

The Brownies nodded to the Queen in acceptance. Sming and Sammo could not believe their luck.

The Queen retired whilst the four had endless snacks, cakes, tea, pies and Snacabitān (apparently, the Queen was still partial to the orange stuff). Anything they asked for was brought to them in a flash. The Brownies, although chirpy, were very professional in their manner and quizzed the Smidgeon on "how Smilad fared", "was Smintagel still plagued by the ghosts of the old knights" and such like.

As the day moved slowly towards dusk, the Queen finally returned with several bottles, some parchment and a bag of what looked like silver pebbles. She handed them all to Ossie de Brunt and whispered in Fiera but neither Sming nor Sammo could make it out.

The Queen bid them safe journey but as they were about to leave she took Sammo to one side and shrunk to speak privately to him.

"Ye have the world in thy hands Sammo. If ye believe, ye canst do anything. Thank ye for helping me to remember who I am. I had forgotten." Then she kissed him on his forehead and Sammo blushed again.

"Godspeed!" she said. "Cama loth Sush Spriggani." she called.

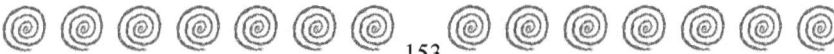

Instantly, a Spriggan appeared to do her bidding.

"Give my guests safe passage to the gateway."

The grey titan held out its mitts and Ossie, Madcap, Sming and Sammo climbed aboard to be escorted from the palace. Out through the gateway into the throbbing woods, back over the swampland and delivered safely in front of the door where Sming and Sammo's journey had first begun.

The great door now stood in the middle of a lush green field, in broad daylight, with nothing in front, behind, at its sides or above it.

"Now which ways did ye come thru?" asked Ossie.

"This way." said Sming pointing to the side of the door they were looking at.

"Ye be deadly sure?" he asked tersely. "Cos we don't wanna be ending up down on the Isle of the Pica or left in the cold at Jeuness!"

"I'm positiva!" yelled Sming.

"'Alrioight! Keep them's wings on yerself! Just checking!" quipped Ossie.

154

Ossie tipped his hat to the Spriggan who opened the door for them. The four walked through. Sming silently prayed to himself that he had got the right direction. As they crossed to the other side the door slammed behind them.

"Well that's that then!" said Madcap looking at Ossie.

It was dark. There was no sign of where they could be. There was a stone underneath their feet with the Fiera markings shining lightly upon it. Then came the sound that Sming had been longing to hear.

"The Ocean!" shouted Madcap "Ye Gods and Gammoric lullabies! I forgot how long tis been since we've seen the Great Ocean Ossie!!" and the two Brownies did a brief little jig before controlling themselves again.

The moon was full, round and low, making ready to concede to her Lord Sun.

Chapter- 13

A stomping good laugh

When Sammo woke the next morning, his head was throbbing and his feet were sore. He remembered that he had dreamt about a most amazing adventure. Selina must have left him to sleep in. The Smidgets were being very quiet (or so he thought) because the world was silent. He closed his eyes for a "two breath" nap when suddenly a big brown furry shape appeared, blocking out the light from the window.

"Be jumblins' Sammo, tis almost Sunupsiddy!" shouted Sming up the stairs as a huge face peered in through the window at him.

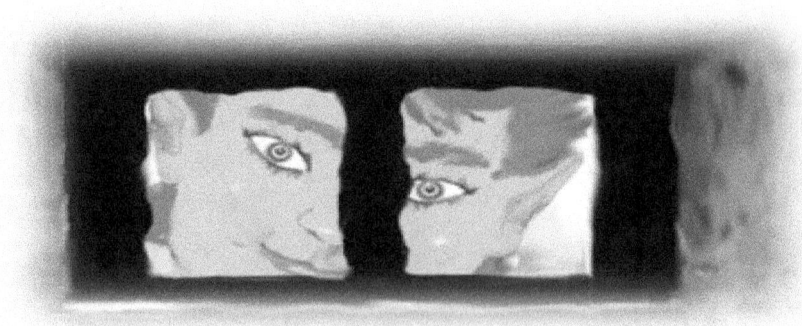

Sammo sprang from his hammock in fright as the events of that night came flooding back.

Madcap gave a cheeky grin and chivied "Come on Sammo! We're to be on our way before long."

Sammo carried out the quickest Sun Dance in Smidgeon history as the sun made its ascent slowly out of the East. Then he rushed downstairs and outside where he found the two Brownies supping piping hot Caithne. There was a slight nip to the air, but Sming said this was often the case in the morning if there was an onshore wind.

Souzette had made a feast for breakfast and the whole of Smintagel chose to eat outside so they could look upon the Brownies. The mood was light and cheery. Even though Smintagel was under no threat from "thems'lot" the return of the Brownies heralded past times.

Ossie and Madcap found they had more new friends than they could count. Everyone had a story about the day the Stars fell, of the Demon God and the glory days when the Færie Queen ruled the world. The whole village was in high spirits until Horatio and Harold of "HeronAir" arrived and then Smintagel's atmosphere dampened.

All that is but Sammo. He was quite excited about travelling on HeronAir as it was not something any of the Smidgeon had ever done. Brownies usually travel by dog but it would have taken too long, so arrangements had been made for a special collection from Smintagel direct to Smilad on Horatio and Harold.

This meant Sammo may be home for Middameal. Sming strapped Sammo onto the tiny seat in front of Ossie de Brunt. Ossie climbed aboard Harold and Madcap boarded Horatio. Sming had a tear in his eye as he said "Goodbyesie" to Sammo. Sammo begged him to come and visit him and see the Smidgets and Selina.

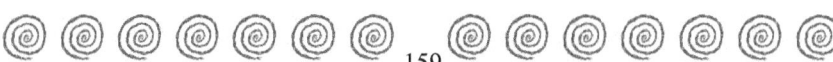

"My 1 haven't seen Sinas in almost a league" he said "1 will visit in Feallan[74] so 1 can watch them prepare the Snacabitan."

"No!" said Sammo "Why putsiofftie when ye can come hither?"

"Mmm" Sming mused to himself. He could find no real reason why he could not return with Sammo, so with a huge beaming smile he chirped "Ye be right me laddo! I'm coming aboard Horatio! Souzel, strap me in!"

Souzel barely had time to strap Sming in and fly hastily down from the heron's back when Horatio clicked his beak. Immediately the herons flew up and off with the Brownies whooping in delight.

With dawn came a thick mist that covered Smilad. It would be another hot day, making the dung bombing hard yet again. The previous day's bombing had not been at all successful and the Smidgeon had been fraught with casualties. Smarahaim creaked in pity for her folk.

74   Autumn.

The four elders, Silures, Sharkey, Stoutnose and Shayle met again that morning to organise yet another rota, taking account of the new casualties.

The Smidgeon schedule is usually a regimented one but it had been abandoned because they were now officially at war. Smidgeon are not a natural warring folk so this was an unsettling time. Even more disturbing was the fact that meal times were all over the place and a hungry Smidge is not a happy one.

The Smidgeon were dropping like flies with many not in a good way. Luckily there had been no fatalities. However, "thems'lot" had used some new kind of rain. A rain that if it was "breevdid in[75]" made a Smidge cough but even "wiersa" if it got onto their skin it "burnstid[76]" more than the Sun at Nonahora.

On the day Sammo left for Smintagel, Sinas had locked himself away and had not been seen or heard from. However, early on this morning, he appeared in the infirmary, checking on those who teetered on the edge of the Summerlands[77], plying them with the special potions he had been making.

---

75   Breathed in.
76   Burned/Burnt.
77   Death.

161

Silures shook his head. Every Smidge that hovered before him looked weak and weary. Sharkey had been assigned with a large group of Smidgeon for the collecting and they looked equally shattered. Most of them stank to high heaven because the dung had permeated their skin, clothes and hair. All in all, Smilad was not a happy place to be.

As the morning drifted into midday, more and more Smidgeon were being treated for burns or coughing fits. Silures came to see Sinas who was running low on potions already.

My Lord, tis getting wiersa! What canne we do? Our people fall like leaves in Feallan[78]…"

"Hush Silures ye will cause chaos should ye falter now. We must bide our time, all rests with Sammo. I hope he be successful or twill be the ruin of us all!" Sinas said shaking his head as he bathed a bald patch on a young Smidge's head where the new rain had scalded him.

"Beoraegn" (pronounced borayne) was the name they had called this new rain. It was in fact an insecticide that Chauncey-Bruff had paid a small fortune for *"to get rid of those midges!"*. "Thems'lot"

---

78 Autumn.

were winning and even Sinas could not see any way out of their predicament.

Now they were officially at war, the Smidgeon had reverted to eating in the Great Hall all together. Selina was helping in the foodheall, making pastry for the pies for Nihealfin which seemed the only meal time that the Smidgeon could come together to eat. Suddenly a shout reverberated through the hall.

"Sammonical returns! Sammo's haim!"

Selina gasped. She was covered in flour but dashed from the Hall, desperate to see her mate. Sure enough, silhouetted against the afternoon sunshine stood two herons, her Sammo (for he was easy to distinguish with his sticky-uppy hair), an old Smidge and two strange looking creatures standing about a foot off the ground dressed in brown fur jerkins, brown leggings and brown fur hats.

"Brownies!" she gasped. "He did it! He really did it!"

As Sammo caught sight of Selina, he ran and pulled her into his arms and kissed her face all over.

Ossie and Madcap looked upon him with knowing smiles.

"That the Missus then Sammo?" Madcap asked.

Sammo nodded and beamed "Aye, this is my Sluf. We've got two Smidgets and lumps on the way." he replied jubilantly so happy to be haim.

"Two or three lumps?" asked Madcap.

"Just the two." Selina replied, smiling with delight that her Sammo was safely haim.

Sinas flew down from the infirmary for not one, but a triple surprise. Sammo had returned safely with Brownies and his brother Sinas. Sinas and Sming danced and embraced each other. It had been a very long time since they had set eyes upon each other.

"Call off the bombing Sharkey!" Sinas shouted to the elder. "Tonight, we revel in victory, for I can smell it is not far beyond the hills!" For the first time in what seemed like an age, Smilad cheered.

Before the party took place,[79] Sinas took counsel with Sammo, Sming, Ossie de Brunt, Madcap Fingle, Silures, Sharkey, Stoutnose and Shayle.

Sinas addressed the Brownies in Boradine, the language of the herd.

---

79   Smidgeon are reknowned for throwing a party for the merest teeniest of excuses!

"Dua căna sonna onth grooo Fiera?" (which means "Do the cows sing in Færie Land?")

Both Ossie and Madcap were impressed by Sinas' knowledge and returned his compliment.

"Ayon. Ouda es căna? (which translated as "But yes. Where are the cows?") asked Ossie.

"Onth grooo an Sonnet ay Nonet onth Ferth." ("By day at grass by night on the Farm.").

"We'll just catch them now Ossie!" said Madcap looking to the sun. "Sammo has told us all of ye troubles. Pray let us give that devil man something to really complain about!"

Ossie urged "Come on Sammo show us the way?"

Sinas nodded his approval to Sammo, who promptly flew off to the fields with Ossie and Madcap in pursuit. It seemed Smilad had ground to halt with the arrival of the Brownies. Smidgets, Smiguts, Smidge and Grumpties alike all piled along behind them to see what the Brownies had planned.

The sun was just past Nonahora. The cows stood swishing their tails and chewing the cud.

"Oh by the Lady herself!" cried Madcap. "Look at thems?! It's worse than ever!" shaking their heads in disbelief, the Brownies ran into the field and only stopped when they were standing behind the herd.

Then Ossie let out a sharp high pitched call.

"Cathamooor!" ("Wake up!").

All the cows all turned to see where the noise came from, with what Sammo could only describe as a look of surprise upon their faces.

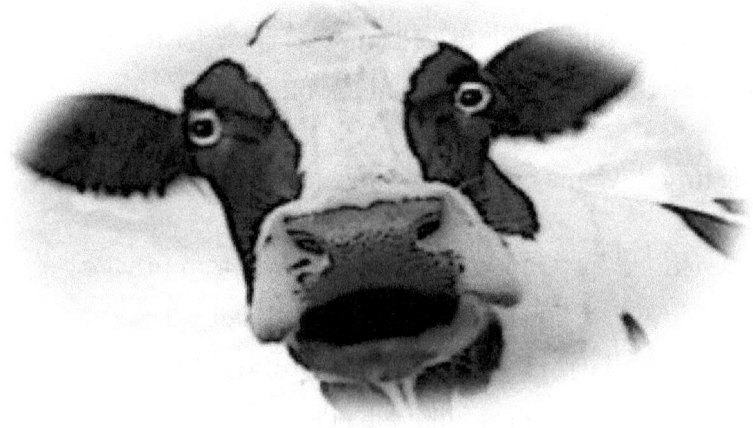

Ossie and Madcap continued toward the cows, who had made a circle around them. Then every cow dropped onto their front knees

while Madcap and Ossie simultaneously touched each cow upon the nose.

"What the blazes?" uttered an unbelieving Chauncy-Bruff as he looked out from one of the windows on his newly built estate.

He scampered out of the house and stood by the stakes that marked the end of the garden boundary. Baffled, he scratched his balding head with his podgy fingers as the cows knelt before the Brownies. Except Chauncy-Bruff could not see the Brownies.

This is because most humans do not believe in Færies (or Sprites in this case) and so therefore cannot (or most likely will not) see them.

Sammo noticed Chauncy-Bruff gawping at the cows. He flew over to Ossie's side, as quietly as he could, so as not to disturb the ceremony.

"The Baas is there!" he whispered into Ossie's ear.

Ossie followed Sammo's finger towards a stout red faced man, who was screwing up his eyes and nose whilst watching the cattle.

"Roight! Time for some shenanigans! Madcap! Look who's come avisiting!"

The pair of Brownies shouted something incomprehensible and the cows all looked to Chauncey-Bruff. Then all of a sudden, every cow began to move toward Chancey-Bruff, slowly at first, until it escalated into a stampede.

Chauncey-Bruff's ruddy cheeks turned pale as he realised the cows were heading directly for him. He ran back into the house but the cows followed him. He ran out the front door and down the lane to where Barrington had parked his limousine but the cows cut him off so he had to run back towards the houses where some of the cows were now waiting swishing their tails. He called out for help. His workman came to see what the trouble was but in turn they too were chased by the cows.

"They've gone crazy!" bellowed Chauncey-Bruff as he ran in yet another direction to elude the menacing herd. "It must be mad cow's disease!"

Sammo, Ossie, Madcap and the whole of the Smidgeon were bent over with laughter as they watched the hilarious antics. How they all guffawed when Sir Rusper almost collapsed with exhaustion, his fat little legs finding it almost impossible to carry him fast enough to escape the herd.

All the while, his men had locked themselves in their workhut and refused to let him.

Chapter- 14

Tearing the house down

There was great revelry in Smilad when the Smidgeon returned from the Greylands. Variations of the story were told to those Grumpties that could not fly far anymore and to the poor souls in the infirmary. The gloomy atmosphere at Smarahaim had lifted and Sammo could sense there was a new optimism in the air again.

At the Smeeting Sinas took the chair as Spechan. He was delighted to introduce everyone to his brother Sming and to the Brownies. Sammo was given a three-ringed salute for achieving a miracle. Then the whole of the Smidgeon joined together outside Ye Old Smidirin for a special Suneall in honour of Ossie and Madcap.

Sinas and Sming were jovial for only a short time before they locked heads together in deep discussion. They decided the Brownies must act that night or they would have to wait a full lunar cycle before the magic could be created again.

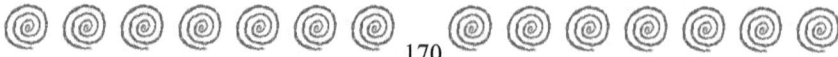

Ossie and Madcap were happy to bide for the month but they sensed the urgency in Sinas' words and so prepared themselves for Nihealf.

Sammo asked if he could help further. Silures who was usually quite offhand with Sammo was now treating him like a son. Silures' behaviour was strange and sentimental. He even patted a suspicious Sammo on the back at one point.

Sinas and Sming assured everyone that it was only Ossie and Madcap that could perform the rite, for the instruction had been given to them and them alone by the Lady Queen. So Smilad retired and Ossie and Madcap got ready for the ceremony.#

As the owls hooted the last call of Nihealf, lights dimmed in the little haims of Smidgeham and Ossie and Madcap weaved their way towards the Greylands.

On reaching the tall shadowed profiles of the housing estate, Ossie turned to Madcap.

"Tis a might eerie with the moon so full beaming her lovely rays upon such a monstrosity don'tchafink Maddy?"

"I do... tis a blemish upon such a magnificent landscape. I was only saying to Buttercup that very thing before that fat fella turned up earlison teedee."

"Ah loverlee Buttercup, I remember her great Grandmooer, Bettina."

"Oh is that her Buttercup now?" asked Madcap.

"Aye. Will ye have drop more of this Snacabitan? Fantastic vintage this year!"

"Twill indeed!"

And the pair of them sat drinking and talking about the cows and generally having a good old chinwag until thin whisp of cloud passed across the pure white moon.

"Begormling Ossie!" cried Madcap. "Is that the time?!. We nigh on nearly missed the slot."

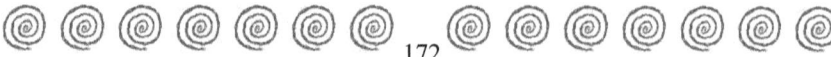

"Whoops!" said Ossie.

By this time, they had both consumed a little too much Snacabitan and with the journey from the Feielands, let's just say the pair of them were slightly worse for wear.

"Have ye got the sintructions?" slurred Madcap.

"Aye have indeed got them - hic!" replied an intoxicated Ossie.

"Shall we have a little dance first to get the magic juices flowing?"

"Ooh I think t'would be rude not to." and they both started to jig, linking arms and singing one of the old songs of the Fiera about the day the Færie Queen thrashed the Demon God.

It was not very long they before they were fairly puffed out.

"Joimping Jiggery, I'm fair pooched. Tis me age, too auld for all this this pokery mingles." gasped Ossie.

'Roight where's that note with her own writing on it?" gasped Madcap.

Ossie pulled the parchment that the Queen had given him from out of an inside pocket.

"And where's the bottles?"

After much clinking and chinking, Ossie produced three phials. One pure white, a bright blue one and one of sparkling silver.

"First ye must find the core?" said Madcap reading from the script. "Oh crikey have ye got a twig of rowan?"

"T'would never leave the Feielands without one – hic!" hiccuped Ossie who then produced a long wand from the rowan tree complete with leaves.

"Eyah! That cannet have been comfortable?" said an impressed Madcap.

174

Ossie tipped an imaginary cap and screwed up his eyes. "Twas not, but tis all for a good cause — hic!" he replied.

They made their way to the new housing estate. Ossie held the rowan twig out in front. He muttered a few words, then sure enough the twig sprung to life. It sparkled and shimmered then took off, dragging Ossie along the ground at great speed before stopping abruptly at the side of one of the houses, pointing downwards, down one of the drains.

"Makes sense." chipped Madcap.

"T'always does. The Rowan is a very reliable source, unlike the Willow too wishy washy!" they both mused.

"Rioght! Repeat after me Ossie!"

"Breekh wareekh, Khikimtha t'away min uthra, rab min kohl, he at-tha, hawlee khaqla karakhem - Tawdee push bashlama" (which roughly translates into "Blessed and be blessed, tis better to have wisdom than wealth, the greatest of all, give her field to her friends. Thank ye and remain in peace.").

Then the two brownies danced around the drain pouring the white liquid into it.

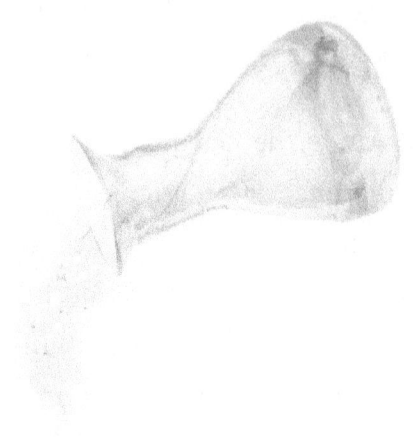

"Ooh not too much she said" chided Madcap.

"Aye but best to make sure..." countered Ossie in return.

As they continued to chant and dance, the remainder of the white liquid went floating down the drain.

"Roight! Now for the blue stuff." said Madcap forging on.

"Aye but let's have 'nother snifter of that jugostuff?" encouraged Ossie.

"Oooh yes, good idea for tis a wee bit caldie round me twinkies!" Madcap motioned to his feet and the pair of them supped more of the Snacabitan whilst jigging like piskies in the moonlight.

"Repeat after meself!" Madcap continued.

"Huadoth, lithbera, Smaradoth, Siolfor, Calter et Argus Aelfkin, bringan neah Wera-cyning, graunter licet freõ pour Eallforis" (which roughly translates to: "Hail to the five tribes of Elf kind, bring forth the Warrior King, grant free licence to the Great Forest.").

Again, Ossie and Madcap jigged around the drain, almost sliding and falling in themselves all the while the blue liquid splashed around as well as running into the drain.

"Oooh not too much of the Aelfbræth!" shouted Ossie. Unfortunately, as the words came out of his mouth, Ossie's feet slid from under him. He grabbed Madcap's arm to steady himself but this resulted in Madcap throwing the phial into the air. They both made a grab to catch it midair but it smashed and trickled down the drain.

"Belumax! That's torn it!" said Madcap, his furry cap was sitting skewwhiff on his head. "Nout for it, t'will all have to go in! Next one Ossilot."

"It's Ossilor!! Creeping Critchers! Get going Fingle before I have your tail!" Ossie feigned irritation.

So off they started again, this time with the silver phial. As they popped out the cork, sparkles of light lifted up into the air. Madcap put his hand over the top of the opening.

"T'always the way with the Fierafür.[80] Come on Ossie, shout harder otherwise it wunna drop intie source!"

"Duadeth couaroth, tonthe maradrang, tensir prenthe, fallack marang, fallack drangam." they both ranted. On the second chant Madcap lifted his hand but still the Fierafür rose upwards so they crouched down and chanted again. Slowly the Fierafür began to cascade and fall.

"'Ye'll have to put it all in!" Ossie said. "T'wont be even otherwise and ye'll end up with some deformities in the land. Trees will start walking and talking then the Lady won't speak to us again! We can't be having that!"

So the whole of the Fierafür phial was poured slowly out. It floated gently on the wind, hovering like Smidgeon before flowing gradually down and into the drain.

"Roight. Last but not leasties! The Fiering. Where be the pebb-lees Ossie my lovely?"

---

80   Fairy Fire.

"Less of the lovely you fool! Ye can save that kinds chitty chat for Missus Madcap!" quipped Ossie raising both his eyebrows whilst handing Madcap a bag of silver pebbles.

"Halftuns." Madcap said pouring half the bag into Ossie's hands.

They each then placed a single pebble, starting at one point, then winding the pebble outwards so that all the silver pebbles made the sign of the Fiera "the Fiering". When Ossie put the final pebble in place, they shouted at the top of their "Manna niowe amendir!" three times. Spinning themselves around and around until they could spin no more they collapsed on the ground.

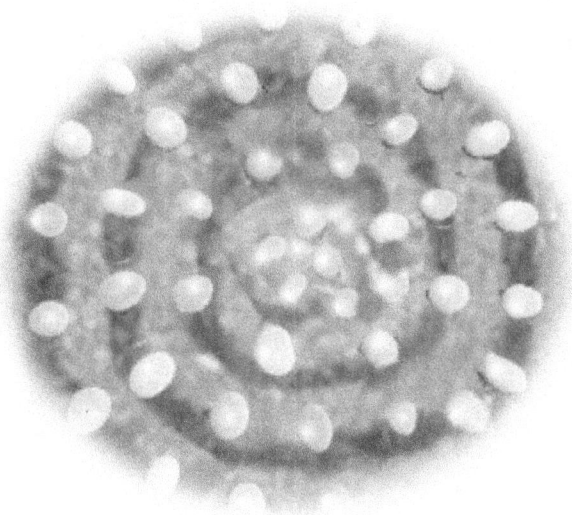

Slowly the pebbles started to glow. Instead of a silvery sheen they shone like stars, burning deep molten white so that it was impossible to see that they were pebbles at all. As quickly as it had appeared so it disappeared, leaving no trace of even a single pebble.

"Tis done." sighed Madcap.

"Great let's have a celebrant!" replied Ossie.

"Good idea!" agreed Madcap.

Few at Smilad had ever slept so well as that night. It was as if a veil of sandy dew dust had been sprinkled in their eyes. No-one heard the banshee-like wails of Ossie and Madcap as they barked at the moon, reciting poems and songs into the early hours of the morning.

Chapter- 15

Back to Business

Sammo woke early. It was dark and for once he had slept a dreamless sleep. Still he could think of nothing except the Greylands and whether Ossie and Madcap had been successful.

Softly he slid out of the hammock without disturbing Selina, who was gently snoozing. He pulled on his clothes and flew down to the living room. For the first time in Sammo's life he found he could not eat.

He was far too excited.

What if he got there and the Greylands had already vanished?

What if they were crumbling at that very moment?

So many thoughts entered his mind as he flew. But his little heart sank when he saw, against the newly rising golden sun, still standing and looming high above, the Greylands, rock solid in front of him.

He gasped. He began to feel himself falling to the ground as the sadness overcame him. His wings refused to work.[81]

Sammo lay upon the soft dewy grass looking at the red tinged clouds thinking "T'will rain today". He had no will to move and cared not if he was trodden on by the cows. There was no point in anything anymore.

"Are ye dead Sammo?" came a broad Boradinian accent.

Sammo blinked to see two brown furry grins looking over him.

"It didney work." Sammo whispered.

"Of course it didney work! Jumping grookles!" sighed Ossie "T'won't happen overnight, we has to wait for nature herself to do the doings."

Sammo perked up. "So it still could work?"

"Course it t'will!" said Ossie and Madcap in unison but with a look of worry upon their faces.

"Now whatcha doin' on yer back?" said Madcap.

---

81   This can happen in very extreme cases where Smidgeon have dolidrumitus ("the dohdrums"). It is still quite a new disease for Smidgeon originating at the turn of the dark ages when the Færies first went into the West.

Sammo's wings began to slowly move again as he pulled himself together. "Oh...oh...oh...I...er...um.... I thought I saw something glistening and flew down to pick it upsie for my Smidgets for the Comeleggie...."

"Roight?" quizzed Ossie, doubting Sammo's explanation, for Ossie sensed it was an unlikely story. However, Brownies are very polite creatures so they both ignored Sammo's fib.

"So when *will* it start?" Sammo asked impatiently.

"Well it could be a day, but then it could be a week..." said Ossie.

"...ah but then it might take a whole season...." chipped in Madcap.

Sammo's shoulders dropped at the thought of having to wait a whole season.

Anticipating Sammo's fragile demeanour, Ossie interjected "Aye, but tis bound to take much less than that." he said pinching Madcap's arm, while Sammo was looking wistfully at the Greylands again.

"Ooooh....Oh aye..." agreed Madcap rubbing his arm "t'will not take that long."

Sammo smiled politely back at them, feeling a slightly more comforted. Suddenly his appetite returned. "Time for Suneall then?" he suggested.

Sammo and the Brownies returned to Smidgham, where Selina was up and pacing the living room.

"Where did ye gets to? I was worried Sluf?!" she probed.

"Sorry Sluf, twas just checking on Greylands."

"Ooh and how is it lookings?" she beamed.

"Still there Sluf, but Ossie and Madcap reckons t'will take a day or so anyways."

"Oh that's good innut? Suneall?" she asked.

"Aye. Better makes enough for Ossie and Madcap too?" suggested Sammo.

"Oooh! Are the Brownies here?" squealed the two little Smidgets appearing from their room.

"They are petsies!" said Sammo, as the two little ones jumped up and kissed him.

"Will ye tell us your tale of the Færie Queen tonight Dada?" asked Sashsi.

"I will petsie, but ye have to be ready for the Bridan soon. Tis buzy-nests today. We return to our usuals."

"Has wars been called off then Sluf?" quizzed Selina.

"Aye, in view of the Brownies and the Færie magik, Sinas called the "Cessare."[82] at the Smeeting. 'sides there are many "Patis"[83], we needed Cessare to get backs up to full strength."

"Enuff talk of warmongering Sluf! Ere' take these to Ossie and Madrigan."

"Tis Madcap!" yelled the Smidgets with glee in their little eyes. They grabbed the dishes from their mother and ran out to see the Brownies.

The Smidgets flew and fussed around Ossie and Madcap who were laughing at both the tiny Smidgets as they tried to carry a huge loaf of bread between them. Everyone had been making gargantuan

---

82   Cease fire.
83   Casualties.

sized portions of loaves, pies and cakes but even so they were still only the size of a finger buffet for the Brownies.

However, the Smidgeon had made enough for a small army, so Ossie and Madcap were constantly undoing the next notch on their belts.

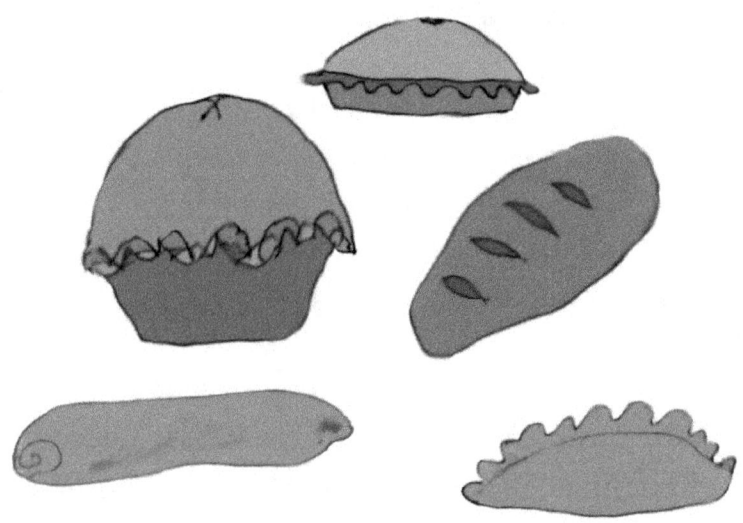

The rest of that day Smilad returned to its daily chores. Sammo's optimism was so high that he left the headgear that Sashsi and Sammus had made for him. Deciding to hold his breath on his return to the Greylands. More's the pity, for the dry rain blasted and the thunder boomed.

After the end of his work, an exhausted Sammo sloped back home. Ossie and Madcap were talking to the cows who seemed to have

taken on completely new personalities. Sammo could hear them singing, laughing and dancing the "Shallie-dun"[84] but Sammo remained melancholy. Selina tried to raise Sammo's spirits by showing him the lumps in her belly thumping as if she had eaten a dozen living rabbits but this seemed to vex him further.

A disheartened Sammo hovered gingerly at the Smeeting. Surprisingly he seemed to be the only one with a troubled soul. All the elders and other Smidgeon were intoxicated with happiness at the sight of the Brownies who now sat watching the Smeeting and drinking Snacabitan from a little barrel.

"Harkety!" came Sinas' voice "Tis time to bid fairetheewell to Ossie de Brunt and Madcap Fingle." Everyone exchanged smiles for glum faces, murmuring their disappointment as the Brownies tipped their fur caps in acknowledgement.

"Aye and not a moment too soon! Before's they drinks' us out of house and haim!" jested Stumble Smidge, the Landlord of Ye Olde Smidirin. The Smeeting burst into laughter and the Brownies raised up their hands laughing heartily.

---

84   An old Bovine dance.

"We wish to thank ye for your help and offer ye a fond goodbysie. Ye will always be welcome and forever will ye be in our hearts."

Once the Smeeting had concluded, the Smidgeon reconvened at Ye Old Smidirin where the word passed around that the Brownies were to leave shortly. Another celebration erupted and fairly finished off that year's supply of Snacabitan. Luckily it was not too long until the harvest at the end of the Fewa.

Sammo could not face the revelry and made tracks for haim. Just as he began his flight a familiar voice called to him.

"Where be ye going laddie?"

"Haim." he replied despondently without even turning to see who it was.

"What's tis the matter Sammo?" came the voice again.

Sammo turned to see both Sinas and Sming smiling back at him. Seeing them standing together he could now see the likeness that had gone unnoticed before. They had the same mischievous twinkle in the eyes, the same silvery skin and same silver hair only Smingel's was slightly longer.

"Are ye twins?" Sammo asked.

188

The pair looked at each other and laughed. "We be!" they said in unison.

"How did I not see it before? Ye be the twins that legend talks of! The ones that fooled all the Magi?"

Sinas and Sming nodded their affirmation.

"But why does Sming live so far South? Why do ye not bide here at Smilad with your brother?"

"The Ley Lines laddo." answered Sming. "The magik of the Smidgeon rely upon the Ley Lines, the lines that bind the old world with the new. Very few Smidge are born with the "Tigãn"[85] but both my brother Sinas and I were. Our Mother was very proud but she knew as soon as we came of age one of us or perhaps even both of us would be sent to another colony."

"Twas luck for me that the Elder passed over on the Fewa that I came of age, whereas poor Sming here was taken to Smintagel..."

"Ah but I have never regretted it and our younger brother Sinton followed for Mother could not bear to think of us all parted and about the world."

"Oh." said Sammo sullenly.

"What it is laddie?" Sming came and shook Sammo by his arms.

"Tis the Greylands..." Sammo sighed.

---

85   The tie that links the ley lines together so the earth magik can flow.

"Ah! Well have faith. Give it time. Smarahaim didney grow in day!" Sming winked at his brother who nodded in agreement but still this did not inspire Sammo.

"I fear it t'will not stop the rains nor the thunder at all!" he moaned.

"Ye must have faith Sammo! If ye didney believe, how did ye expect the majik to work? All magik needs is trust, assurance and belief!" said Sming.

"Tell me this Sammo..." interjected Sinas "...do ye think our Lord Sun will rise tomorrow?"

"Aye of course the Lord Sun will rise..."

"But why of course?" pressed Sinas.

"B...Be... Ber... Because it always rises..." Sammo suggested.

"Ah but do ye not think that is because ye believe? If ye stopped believing it may not!"

"Where's the sense in that?" asked Sammo sulkily.

"Go haim Sammo. Rest your head. Tis been long long days of latsie, best ye allay." suggested Sinas.

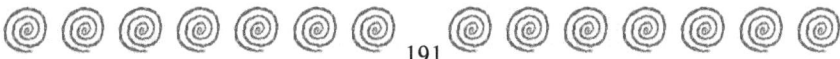

As Sammo flew off into the Twisk, Sinas and Sming watched him go. They shook their heads. Sammo, who once seemed the staunchest of Smidgeon had lost his faith. Sming could no longer celebrate either and he felt his wings flutter in trepidation for Sammo's wellbeing.

Chapter- 16

Coming ready or not!

Sammo rose before Sunrise to find his heart heavier still. The Smidgets were gloomy too, they were going to miss Ossie and Madcap dreadfully and so refused to raise a single smile not even a burpy one. It seemed to Selina that she was the only chirpy Smidge at haim and felt sure her family had been replaced by a group of "mumpters"[86].

"Oooh ye moozie mumpters!" she yelled. "Be gone from my kitchen afore I sweep ye up and puts ye in the Eallpool to wash away those mumpty frowns!!"

Sammo flew languorously out of the door to begin his day as a Comeleg. The Smidgets grouched further, while Selina tidied their hair and washed away spots of moochi from around their mouths, before she delivered them to the Bridan.

---

86   Small angry insects that do nothing but hiss and grunt.

Nothing had changed that was true but the general ambience of Smilad and its surrounding landscape was still one of jauntiness. The Brownies seemed to have brought some of the "auld magik" with them but now, it was time for them to leave. Their "farewell party" had been a messy event. There were barrels of empty Snacabitan strewn everywhere. Every larder was empty. Even the half-eaten pies and stale loaves had been consumed. It was as if a swarm of woodworm had seen a newly carved chair and hacked their way through it.

At two breaths past dawn, Sinas and Sming made ready to say goodbye to Ossie and Madcap. Ossie pulled his Rowan twig from out of his pocket and mumbled the Færie passwords. Sure enough, the twig flew into action dragging Ossie behind. Sinas and Sming looked on with a mischievous look upon their faces as the twig came to an abrupt halt at Smarahaim. Ossie scratched his head and looked from Madcap, to Sming, to Sinas and then back to Madcap.

"Can't be roight?" he said.

"Ah-hem! Master Ossilor, I think you'll find ye have safe passage here." said Sinas.

"But tis Smarahaim, tis ye's haim?" Ossie said scratching his head again.

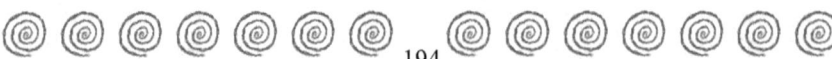

"Can ye not see the mark? Perhaps if ye take a few steps back?" advised Sinas.

Ossie and Madcap took a few steps back, peered sideways at Smarahaim, then gasped. Sure enough in the centre of her trunk was the winding mark of the Fiering, the Færie Ring.

"Tee hee!" chuckled Ossie. "Would ye believe her?!"

"No wonder the Lady is so fond of ye Smarahaim. Ye be one of the auld clan!" yelped Madcap.

"So how cam ye never came through this ways?" said Ossie pulling on his chin.

"This way is forbidden for the Smidgeon. We made our choice long ago." said Sinas solemnly, offering no further explanation.

The Brownies continued to chortle to themselves amazed that they had never realised that Smarahaim was one of the original trees of old. Soon, they became solemn and forlorn. It was time to leave. Madcap uttered the secret passwords. The spiral mark at Smarahaim's centre began to shine and grow. The Brownies walked towards the ring, where now there was a pathway that offered them passage back to the Feielands. Slowly they wound themselves around and deeper into the ring until finally they faded out of sight. Sming and Sinas sighed and smiled, both knowing exactly what the other was thinking.

"Tidy upsie me thinks?!" said Sinas.

"Aye." nodded Sming.

The day progressed into Nonahora, then into Twisk and before long another day was over. A downhearted Sammo became more

distraught with each passing day. His sleep was restless. He tossed and turned, dreaming only of the Greylands. In his mind, the Færie Queen had completely deserted them.

When he woke on the third day, the Sun could not be seen for dark heavy clouds. Sammo's hopelessness hit an all-time low. Luckily, for Selina, the Smidgets had cheered up. They tried to rally Sammo along, while she fed him copious amounts of Moochie, all in the vain hope that Sammo would "buck up and be a rabbit", but to no avail.

Come Middameall, Sammo was inconsolable. He point blank refused to visit the Greylands for fear of the worst. Selina sent for Sinas. Both Sming and Sinas came. They had also lost their happy outlook and looked to Sammo's mood as a portent.

A "S'late Smeeting" was called and even Silures and Sharkey felt worried for poor Sammo. He had been right all along about the Greylands, could he still be right now? Everyone left the S'late Smeeting feeling almost as dejected as Sammo.

As the next few days passed. Sammo refused to eat, sleep, fly or do anything. He took to his hammock. Selina sat by his side genuinely fearful.

"He has an ague." she wept as Silures, Sinas and Sming came to tend to him. "I have never seens him like this!"

The Elders shook their heads. They had never seen a fever like it before. It was as if Sammo was willing himself into the Summerlands.

The weather outside was unlike any weather the Smidgeon had seen for the time of year. Hail stones the size of Smiguts, thick black clouds, heavy showers of rain, lightning and thunder. Even Sming and Sinas agreed that it was as if the world was coming to an end.

Sammo was delirious. He ranted in his sleep, sweat pouring from his brow. "The magika dunney work, she has no power here... the magik means nuffinks.... the ley lines are disparages...the Lady cannot help us...there is no love left in the world..."

Sming and Sinas fretted.

"What if he *is* right?" worried Sming.

"Tis nothing but deridreaming! Dunnat ye start. We'll have an Nihealfin Smeeting for the whole Smidgeon. We must get the magik working again. P'raps he be right about the line, could it be disparaged? Who bides in your place? fretted Sinas.

"Souzel? He's my successor."

"Mmmm. Well tis worth a return to the West for ye. I'll speak to Skylark and see if he'll take ye all the way seeing as urgenties."

Meanwhile the rain and hail drove wildly on. The sun vanished for nearly three days.

But one good thing happened.

The weather seemed to stop the building work at Greylands. Silures had even ventured there himself, he was so fraught for Sammo's return to health.

On his visit there, the rain came down so hard he had to ask a mole to take him through one of his mole hole passages so he could look upon Greylands. Silures and the kindly mole made three attempts of "coming up" before Silures eventually got a quick but very blurry view.

The good news was there was no noise, no dry rain and none of "thems'lot". He relayed all this to a comatosed Sammo. Selina who had remained constantly by Sammo's bedside gave Silures a grateful yet grief stricken smile.

Skylark arrived and so it was time for Sming to return to Smintagel to check on the Ley Lines. As he said his goodbyes, both he and Sinas shed a tear. Then they slapped each other on the arm and feigned humour, for neither of them knew whether they would see each other again before they passed over into the Summerlands.[87]

As agreed by Sinas, Skylark would carry Sming all the way back to Smintagel. Unsteadily he took off through the mysterious driving wind and rain that clung uncannily to the base of only the surrounding lands of Smilad and the Greylands. Once Skylark had

---

managed to stagger through the black clouds they were greeted with brilliant sunshine and the journey was a swift one.

Four further days of heavy rain and hail followed. There was no sign of Sammo ever breaking from his fever. Sinas prepared Selina for the worst, but she tried to remain hopeful.

Finally, Sinas took her aside from the Smidgets, who were busy brushing Sammo's red hair whilst telling him the story of "Scancalang and the Horseradish".

"There be nish I can give him. Our magik falls flat and fails my dear. Tis as if he has given up the will of the Smidgeon."

"Nonsense my Lord! I know Sammo, he will snapsidandy[88] soon. Sammo wunnat leave us, not so soonas." she smiled refusing to listen to such pessimism.

"Tis full well ye know my dear that if his wings dunnat beat in the next day then they'll beat no more..." Sinas whispered with tears in his eyes. "I dunnat want to scare ye but all is done that canne be donst and I canne think of anythings to get him going. Can ye?" pleaded Sinas.

---

88   Break out of it.

Selina shook her head and wept softly so the Smidgets could not hear her. Her lumps beat against her stomach and made her gasp for breath.

"What ails ye my dear?" Sinas held her arm as she winced again.

"Tis the lumps, they be banging to come! They are leagues early mind?"

"Can happen in times of grief" said Sinas helping Selina to her rocking chair. "I'll get ye something to calm them."

"But I have still two moon cycles yet?!"

Sinas looked her over.

The signs said the twins were ready.

There was nothing more he could do for Sammo especially now Selina needed him.

Chapter- 17

What kinda magik d'yer call that?!

Sammo was dreaming, or was he?

He was back in the Færie Wood, walking around and around in circles. He could not find his way into the middle. He could not find the stones. He wanted to tick the Færie Queen off. She had promised him that she would help but she just pretended and piled them off with a couple brown rats and some stew in a pot that he was still holding.

He began to shout.

"Oi! Oi!! Oi!? Where are ye? Ye usurper!! Ye auld witch! Ye hag of hellfire!" he cursed and cursed.

"What is all this noise Sammonical!?" shrieked a very small Færie Queen.

"Ye bejiggered me, conned me outta me wings for nout! Now all I have is stew and rats and no way haim well no haim to gets to anyways! What ye gonna do about it?!"

The Færie Queen laughed at him. "Oh Sammo ye are so dafty sometimes, but I do adore ye. Come tis not a place for ye to bide. Sabine and Sabin are jumping up to meet you."

"Oh they'll be fine. I canne be doing anything but this stew...."

"Oooh no Sammo, they need ye more now than ever! The stew will dry out before ye get home trust me, have I let ye down before..."

And before he had time to answer her, there was a great clamour of light and sound.

"... get the rope... bring fresh water... Silures, Silus... these mumpters are hell bound if ye dunnat move!" came a familiar voice.

Sammo's eyes woke to darkness. He could smell strange ointments and candles were lit and burning in every corner of the room.

"My Goodness1" Sammo thought "...have I passed over to the Summerlands already....?"

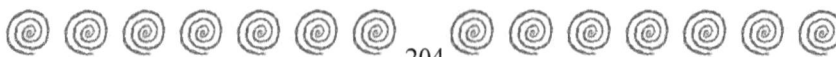

Sammo tried to move his wings but they would not budge. He tried to move his legs but they would not move either. He then thought "...start at the top and work down Sammo me boy...". So he wiggled his nose and it worked! Then he opened his mouth and chomped his teeth. My my, he felt hungry. His tummy turned over for it was so empty. Then he tried his fingers, his toes and eventually he was moving again. He crawled out of the hammock and opened the beddrum door to see chaos below him.

Selina was laid out and had seven Magi working around her.

"Oh my fribblings! The Lumps!" he mouthed to himself.

All of a sudden, his wings sprang to life, the tingles came back to his twinkle toes and he cared no longer whether the Greylands were there or not. His Sluf and his lumps needed him and was very sure he was going to be there.

"Sammo!" shouted Selina.

"Sammo!" shouted a delighted Sinas, Silures and Silus.

"No time!" said Sinas.

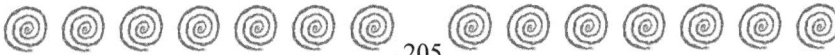

"I know! Twas the same with Samus! Nasty little wrigglers our Smidgets, here let me!" and Sammo got to work on Selina. He bent her forward flew her upright.

"I'm not sure that's quite right?" said an anxious Sinas.

"Be fines!" Sammo said, soon out of breath.

And it was.

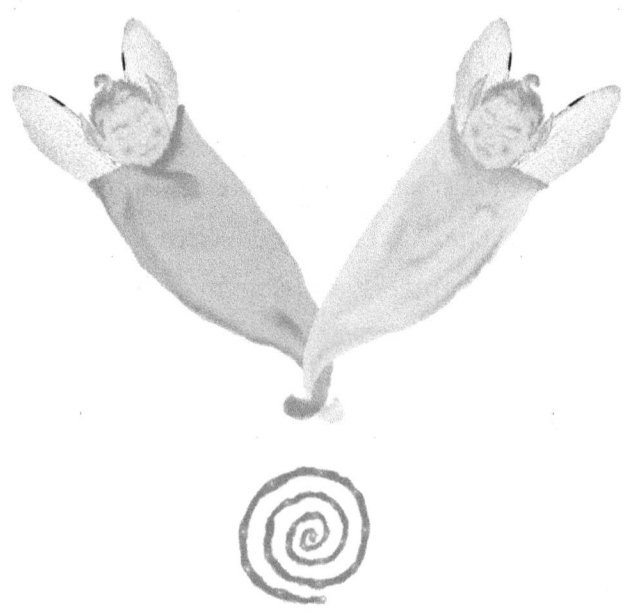

Chapter- 19

Here comes the sun!

At the break of dawn, so came the first golden morning in Smilad for a long time. Soft gilded rays drenched the sodden earth and beamed through the window of the haim of Sammo just as the first cry of Sabine could be heard, followed closely by the squeaking gurgle of Sabina.

"Oh Sammo!" cried Selina. "I knew ye wouldney miss their first Sonsonet."

"Corsnot Sluf!"

Sammo pressed his head to Selina's looking down at the two smallest Smidget babies Smilad had ever seen.

Sinas nodded to the Magi Elders who kindly understood it was time for them to leave.

"Sammo." Sinas said softly. "Tis good to have ye back."

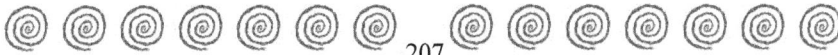

"Mmmm...I dunna where I went... but tis good to be haim."

Sammo rushed around as if he had never been unwell, but by mid-morning he was quite pooped. Sashsi and Samus returned haim as they had been staying with their Grumpties, so all of the relatives came to see the tiny twins.

Sammo was happy.

He realised it did not matter what "thems'lot" tried to do to the world. As long as the Smidgeon were in it there would always be magik and as long as he had his family he could make it through anything.

As the rest of the family cooed over the new arrivals, Sammo decided to get some fresh air.

He needed to spread his wings, for they felt like frozen cardboard. He had not intended to go to the Greylands but his wings were stiff and it was second nature for him to travel there.

There was a lot of commotion when he arrived. Many of "thems'lot" were shouting. Chauncy-Bruff's face was even brighter red than usual as he stood and pointed his finger at a man in a hat, who was holding some very strange implements.

Alongside them were some funny looking types of "thems'lot", all dressed in bright colours.

Sammo looked bemusedly at the scene before him, not really thinking too much about what was going on. He had made the decision that it was time to let be what must be. He had been lost but now he knew what was really important.

As he watched the hubbub, he dipped into a daydream of Selina and the Smidgets when a voice came.

It took him quite by surprise.

"Sammo?" she said.

"Aye!" he said jumping out of his skin, looking around hesitantly. He knew the voice but he could not remember who it belonged to.

"Sammo? Here behind ye." she urged.

Sammo turned around slowly to see the Queen of the Færies standing by an old crooked tree that he had never noticed before, despite coming this way over many moons and seasons.

"My Ladyship!" he said bowing lowly.

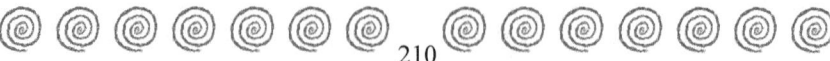

"Very good but get ye up! I'm glad ye made it haim. Twas a worry for me for a while, ye roaming the woods miggling. Ye Gods 1 thought ye'd never go!!" she laughed her soft lulling laugh.

"Er sorry?" he said reddening and remembering his dream or perhaps it had not been a dream after all.

"Do ye know what is happening?" she said pointing to Chauncy-Bruff and the ever-growing crowd.

Sammo shook his head and shrugged his shoulders.

"Come with me." she ordered.

Sammo flew onto her hand and she whisked him besides the crowd.

"Don't worry they canne see ye." she reassured, as she blew on him very gently. All of a sudden Sammo could understand everything they were saying.

"...I'm telling you now! You either get off of Bruff Property or I'll have my lawyer sue you for everything..."

"...and I'm telling you Mr Chancey-Stuff that if you don't pull this lot down by mid afternoon tomorrow I'll slap an injunction on you

so fast that Bruff Homes will never be seen this side of Swaleford again!"

A huge cheer went out from all the colourful people.

"This is preposterous!" Chancy-Bruff ranted "What right? I have planning permission..."

"You did, but now you don't. It's been revoked. This land is listed. These kind folk found the old plans and ruins of an ancient Druidic settlement and the Government have given them full grants to excavate. Your estate is bang on the top of it, so I suggest you help them or you'll end up in Smartfield Prison".

The man in the hat started to walk away and Chauncy-Bruff followed after him shouting insults and getting redder with each breath.

Sammo beamed "But what about this lot?" he said pointing to the odd-looking people who were smiling and hugging each other.

Ah the colourful ones. The freewillers. They are the last remaining hope of Mankind, Sammo. The saviours of the land. Some of them have very distant heritage to Aelfkin, my children the Elves. It is in them that we must rest our hope for truth."

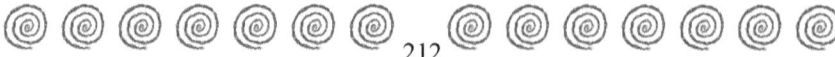

"So, the Greylands...."

"Will be torn down and this land will return to verdancy once again. The trees are safe, the grass will grow high and no one will ever dare to tread on Smidgeon terrain again.

"So ye did do it!" cried Sammo jumping into a backflip and then cartwheeling in the air.

The Færie Queen smiled and laughed a happy laugh. One of the colourful people looked over at them as if he could see something but he shrugged and looked away.

"Come Sammo tis not safe now. Besides, I have a present for ye." she whispered then ushered him from her hand. She then shrank to his size and hovered, much to Sammo's surprise, as the Færie Queen had no wings.

But his attention shifted to her hand, something sparkled and he saw that she was holding out a silver object. It was a small round pendant that hung upon the most delicate silver chain. Upon one side of the pendant the Fiering had been engraved and on the other side was Sammo's name etched in Fiera.

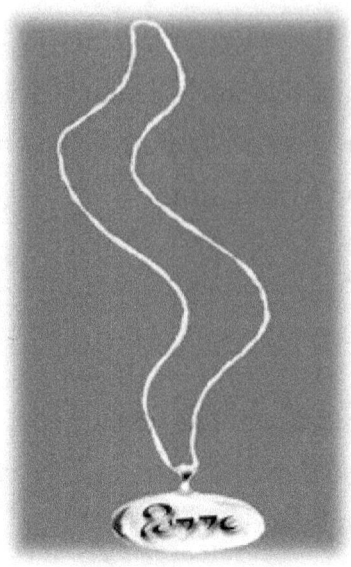

"Ye are a strange Smidge, Sammo, for ye found a way back into the Feielands without any magik, as if ye willed yeself. So, I give ye this pendant. Should ye need me, rub the spiral and it will bring you to the centre of the Færie wood to the stone by my throne."

Sammo gasped and smiled.

"But hear this too! Do not use this gift lightly nor tell another soul. Tis only for ye. Harken that it works both ways for if I have need of ye I can pull thee as I choose." And she laughed a mischievous laugh.

"B...be... ber... but wunnat folk ask about it?"

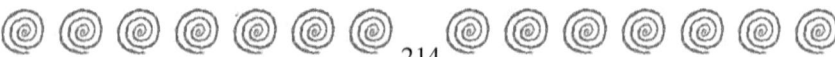

"Canst only be seen by ye and mine eyes alone. Tis a Færie talisman, canst only be worn by ye or taken by me."

Sammo looked at the pendant and felt a sense of pride.

"Now get back to those brand new Smidgets for they will be more of a handful than ever Sinas and Sming were!"

The Færie Queen grew to her full size again, walked to the old crooked tree and vanished.

Sammo was sorry to see her go. The Sun seemed to shine so brightly wherever she was. He looked down at the pendant in contemplation, then pulled himself together before flying haim.

Selina was being fussed over by everyone. She was mighty glad to see Sammo because the Grandparents, Grandtyparents and Grumpties were making such a racket they were fairly driving her insane. Sammo kissed her and made her comfy before coaxing everyone out of the door.

Sinas came to visit shortly before the Smeeting and Sammo felt sure he could sense something different about Sammo but Sinas said nothing. Sammo watched Sinas' every move, checking to see whether he could see his new pendant, but Sinas seemed oblivious. Sammo even played with it, hanging it over his vest as he sat directly

in front of Sinas. The Queen had been true to her word, no-one could see it. Not even one of the Magi!

Then Sammo remembered the great news!

"Oooh, the Greylands!" he yelped as Sinas began to make ready to leave for the Smeeting.

"Greylands?" asked Sinas.

"Aye, they're being torned down!"

Sinas gasped in disbelief.

"Ye know this?"

"Aye take ye there myself so ye can see with own eyes?"

Sinas and Sammo flew out to the Greylands. Sure enough, the Freewillers were still there. Notices were being put over the Gateway and in the windows of each of the houses had new signs in them that said:

"Condemned! Site of archaic and ancestral excavation."

Sinas flew to the Gateway to read the small print. His smile widened with each word, beaming from ear to ear. It was true. He grabbed Sammo and kissed him and danced.

"Ye did it my boy! Ye did it!!"

Chapter- 19

Celebrantes!

The Smeeting lasted a record two breaths that Twisk. It was just enough time for Sinas to call the "Harkety!" and to say "the Greylands was soon to be gone forever" before the entire congregation of Smilad flew off to celebrate in Ye Olde Smidirin.

"Forever" is a long time thought Sammo.

Certainly almost as long as the hot dusky night that seemed to go on and on that eve.

That day was written into Smidgeon legend. "Thems'lot" were foiled because one little Smidge refused to give in.

Sammonical Smidge was honoured in the only way a Smidge could be. He was fed every concoction known to Smilad. The festivities lasted nearly three whole days and would have been longer, but for the Snacabitan running dry, for which the Brownies took the blame.

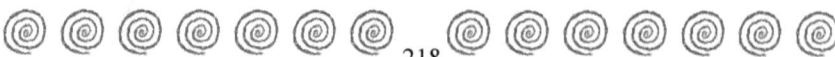

The whole of Smilad sung, drank and prayed to the Færie Queen to keep Sammonical Smidge safe in her arms forever.

...but we know she will, don't we?

The End

Glossary

Word	Meaning
Ælfbræth	Blue liquid. A potent and magic liquid taken from the Bræth dua Ælf, a waterfall found in the realm of Fiera
Baas	The Boss. Leader. Head of the Clan
Baasdom	Big boss-like behaviour
Bacas	Bakers
Bandroms	The stringed instruments made from sticks and stems of leaves and acorns, played either as guitar, banjo, lute, mandolin, fiddle or double bass, depending on the number of strings. Strings are kindly donated by the forest animals. Usually a set of whiskers from a dead relative said to bring the deceased's family good luck and easy winters
Beddrum	Bedroom
Beorægn	Insecticide
Biænben	The Binding Cup. A festive cup that binds the Smidgeon together at Micælmas
Blæcwicca	Black Magic
Booties	Shoes
Boradine	The language of cows usually spoken by Brownies.

Word	Meaning
Boviedrinca	Milk
Bovies	Cows
breevdid in	breathed in
Bridan	Bus Stop
Brownie	A Brownie is a sprite, a member of the Feie Spirite who serve the Færie Queen. Most Brownies stand between 1 to 2 feet tall. They are herdsfolk and maintain the herds, fields and lands as well as keeping peace and order with their earth magic.
Buckas	Wailing large nether creature from the time of Merlin, not seen for many years but are thought to still live below in the darkness of the caves under Tintagel
Buculus	The Horn of War
Bugs of War	See "Werrebuck"
burnstid	Burned/burnt
buzy-nests	Extremely busy
Byldis	Builders
Caithne	The leaves of the Strawberry Tree dried to make teas and herbs. The Strawberry Tree is only found in ancient English and Irish woodland so has to be delivered by Chiff Chaff or Wigeon in return for a barrel of Snacabitān
Calling	Three "whoots" followed by one "whoohoo" followed by a further three "whoo whoo

Word	Meaning
	whoohoohoos" hooted by owls to mark Nihealf (Midnight)
Capari	Fishermen
Casus	Cheese
Cessare	Cease fire
Chareeto	Car/chariot/vehicle
Comelegs	Collectors
Croakles	Old age
Da Da	Dad
Dawnmeall	Breakfast
Dohldrums	A very extreme case of dolidrumitus. Quite a new disease for Smidgeon originating at the turn of the dark ages when the Færies first went into the West.
Doolally Dew	A fine silvery dust and the Smidgeon's greatest weapon against "thems'lot". One puff of doolally dew in the face of one of thems'lot can induce sneezing fits, followed by feeling of lightheadedness, a "tipsy" sensation, as if you had supped one too many glasses of your Grandma's sherry that she keeps for trifles and special occasions but you're quite happy, slightly queezy and you think everything is marvellous, can't possibly remember your name or where you live but your Mother is due to collect you and you could do with a nice nap by the side of a babbling brook

Word	Meaning
Dust	Dry rain / dust created by human builders.
Eallpool	The communal pool where all the Smidge bathed
Ealu	Drink made from berries taken from the Chequer tree
Elcargo	Money
Escheat	Trickster
Feallan	Autumn
Feie Gomshum	Idiot
Feie Spirite	The Sprite Family
Fewa	Summer
Fewamagist	Master for the Year
Fiera	The language of the Færie Queen
Fieradu	Fairy Dew – the drink of the Færies – a bit like very sweet tea
Fierafûr	Fairy Fire. A magic potion only made by fiera magik
Fierakaka	Small cakes. Ironically, Fierakaka are fairy cakes so called by "thems'lot" back in the old days when Færies and Man lived hand in hand. The Færies brought King Arthur cakes when he miraculously pulled Excalibur from the stone. Arthur loved them so much he begged the Færie Queen to give his cook the recipe and thenceforth named them Fierakaka "Fairy Cake"
Flearoll	Flea wrapped up in potato and cheese

Word	Meaning
Fountainheart	Village Square
Freewillers	Last of the line of Ælfkin.
Fribblings	A term used to express shock or annoyance.
Fromies	Dairy Folk
Gamas	Keepers of the Woods
Gatcas	Cheese (like goats' cheese)
Gatcas Toasties	Cheese on Toast
Goodly Biniht	Goodnight
Grandtyparents	Great Grandparents
Greylands	Human Housing Estates and built up areas
Grubs Up	Cooked grub, belly up, so its legs stick out of the pastry
Grumpty(ies)	Very very old Smidgeon
Haim	Home
Haims	Smidgeon Houses
Harkety!	Listen up! Harkety! is used at the start of every notice at a Smeeting.
Horasnack	Later afternoon tea
ickmush	Selfish
iree	Angry and disrespectful
Lumps	Unborn Smidge babies
Magi	Head of Smidgeon, maker of magik
Magisters	Deciders of the Lore
Magus	Teacher, magik maker, magik breaker, upkeeper of the Smidgeon faith and lore

Word	Meaning
Mansprek	The language of humans
Micælmas	The last day of December, like Christmas Day
Midafora	Teatime in the afternoon.
Middameall	Lunch
Mitters	Messengers
Moochi	Made from ground hazelnuts and honey, it tastes like chocolate and Smidge spread it on toast
Moondancers	Fireflies
Mooty	Nasty
Mumpters	Small angry insects that do nothing but hiss and grunt
Narkinstuff	Chemical waste
Nihealf	Midnight
Nihealfin	Midnight Feast.
Ninohundrid-ninonino	999 years old, a much-celebrated birthday
Nonahora	High Noon
Nonamuch	Early afternoon tea
Nut Toasties	Moochi covered bread
Patis	Casualties
Perfectamundo	Absolutely perfect
Petsie	Love, Mate (term of endearment)
Pinkies	Hands

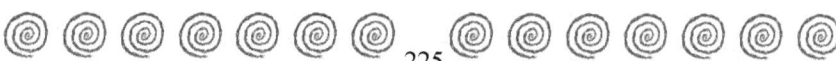

Word	Meaning
Piradee	The Smidge funeral where the moonflies carry the wrapped body and set fire to it above the river
Piskies	Pixies
Plegadabord	A table game involving as many players that you wish but at least 2, the more the players the more difficult. The table is the board. A player has a home (like Ludo) and must make it through the board rolling an octagonal dice (if you get 8 you roll again). It's a bit like snakes and ladders to get to the middle. The last one to get there wins the game which is typical of Smidgeon who always do everything backwards
Pou-da-dew	A pouch is attached to every Smidgeon belt, from the day they breathe air containing doolally dew
Prim	Primspechan – the Head Speaker
Quackers	Doctors
Scancalang	A Smidge who was as tall as his legendry tales
Searall	Elevenses
S'farva	Father, Dad
Shallie-dun	An old Bovine dance, danced by cows when they are happy
Sluf	Darling, Sweetheart. A term of endearment
Smarantee	Tea made from the leaves of the Chequer tree

Word	Meaning
Smeeting	The nightly meeting of Smidgeon where the events of that day are debated and discussed. Announcements, such as, births, deaths, marriages and engagements and most importantly, the disturbing and ever-changing ecosystem of Smilad.
Smidge	A very small creature, usually between 3-4 centimetres (in some very rare cases like Scancalang, who measured a whopping 5 centimetres)
Smidgeon	The Smidge en mas; the collective of Smidge
Smidgets	Babies and Toddlers
Smigut	Teenager
Smilad	The ancient lands of Smidgeon consisting of four districts:
	Smidgewick
	Smidginton
	Smidgeham
	Smarahaim
S'muvva	Mother, Mum
Snacabitan	Drink made from berries taken from the Chequer tree with adders' venom added to it, very potent
Snapsidandy	Break out of it
Sonsonet	An ancient song passed down from the Fiera in the original language of the Gods, sung in

Word	Meaning
	celebration of the creation of the world by the Sun God Ramunil
Spechans	Callers at the Smeeting
Spithrasiol	Silk spun by spiders which is knitted into garments worn by Smidgeon
Sranjey	Soft drink made from the berries of the Chequer tree
Stickleback pie	Pie made with sticklebacks from the river
Stringans	Musicians and Singers
Summerlands	The place where Smidge go once they die. Also, Summerlands refer to "death"
Suneall	Sunset meal
Sunippy	Daytime
Sunupsidown	All day (sun up to sun down)
Sunupsiddy	Quite a few breaths past dawn
Thems'lot	Humans
Tigãn	The tie that links the ley lines together so the earth magik can flow
Tromme	A large Drum that is banged upon to commence and finalise a Smeeting
Twinkies	Toes
Twisk	Evening time, just before Dusk
Twisker	The Speaker for the Eve
Tyrstups	Upstart

Word	Meaning
Werrebuck	A strange looking creature that dwells within the depths of Smarahaim. Bound to protect her and the Smidgeon
Wiersa	Weird and bad
Woody Pot	Thick steamy stew made from woodlice with fluffy dumplings